P9-DXG-404

Bitter Lake

MARIKA DELIYANNIDES

BITTER LAKE

The Porcupine's Quill

Library and Archives Canada Cataloguing in Publication

Deliyannides, Marika, 1968–, author
    Bitter Lake / Marika Deliyannides.

ISBN: 978-0-88984-374-5 (pbk.)

    I. Title.

PS8607.E48275B58 2014   C813'.6   C2014-903973-5

Published by The Porcupine's Quill, 68 Main Street, PO Box 160,
Erin, Ontario NOB 1T0. http://porcupinesquill.ca

Edited by Chandra Wohleber.

Represented in Canada by Canadian Manda.
Trade orders are available from University of Toronto Press.

We acknowledge the support of the Ontario Arts Council and the Canada Council
for the Arts for our publishing program. The financial support of the Government
of Canada through the Canada Book Fund and the Government of Ontario
through the Ontario Media Development Corporation is also gratefully
acknowledged.

For Dad

One

I am trapped in my car.

Mid-afternoon.

A day so muddled by the grey sky that it appears winter is coming, not going.

A day at odds with itself.

I've been this way for over an hour, an uneasy hostage fettered by the steering wheel as my car moves me closer to my destination. A glaze of sweat dampens my upper lip; my stomach tightens in a queasy knot. I take a deep breath and hold it in my lungs. Is there any journey so filled with apprehension as the one that leads you home?

It's as though a greater force, something manipulating me beyond my better judgment, has reached out its meddling hand to pluck my black Honda Civic from its regular city life and deposit it on this rural highway, where cars move forward cautiously through the sleet of the early Alberta spring. The highway is an assembly line, and I'm just one piece of the moving creation, to be spit out only when my final shape has been realized.

The reason for my reluctance is no mystery—

Seven days ago, my sister, Dorothea, phoned from Concord, where she lives with my parents and her eight-year-old son, Ryan. She was calling about my parents' move to the Vista Grande Retirement Villa. 'So are you coming to help?' she asked, speaking too loudly as usual.

I pictured her at the beige wall phone in the kitchen of our old home with its worn checkerboard floor and avocado-green fridge, frowning as she looked out the large picture window bordered by ruffled curtains. Or perhaps she was in the downstairs rumpus room on the rust-brown velour sectional sofa, chosen by our mother years ago to match the knotty brown macramé plant hangers that had long been purged of their dried-up ferns.

'I'll see what I can do.' A coward's response.

She saw through it, of course. 'So that means no?' She snorted. 'It figures!'

'For Christ's sake, don't act as though you're the only one who ever shows up.' Her voice rattled me, as it always did. Because she is deaf in her left ear from a deformity known as cauliflower ear (a condition usually reserved for professional boxers), she's prone to talking in a near yell.

'Well show up then, and give me a hand. These boxes aren't going to pack themselves.'

'Our bathroom's in the middle of being retiled,' I objected, cutting into a bag of plaster with a utility knife.

'I've got Ryan to look after and my midterms are coming up. Anyway, I do enough around here.'

I clutched the knife in my hand. I'd taken on another home-renovation project, keen to replace the old black ceramic tiles, which constantly needed to be wiped clear of water spots. 'Are you kidding me?' Calvin had said when he came home to find boxes of limestone tiles stacked like a dam in the front hall. 'Should you even be lifting those boxes?'

Dorothea's shrill voice twisted my insides out. I owed my sister—and not just for the crumpled, useless ear. The childhood accident that caused the disfigurement was only a precursor. I could hardly refuse her request to come home. 'Okay,' I acquiesced, sliding the blade back into its sheath. 'I'll be there.'

The feeling of claustrophobia grows as I near Concord.

Through the car's windshield the snowflakes are haphazard and fierce. A snow globe of a scene with its simple landscape: a picture-perfect evergreen here, a quaint farmhouse there, the moody mouse-grey sky—a neat, if oppressive panorama that has been my only view on the highway for nearly a hundred miles.

The only exit (the only way *out*) would be the narrow gravel driveways that lead to the quaint farmhouses where bushes grow as sturdy and resolute as sentries against the stucco-sided homes, guarding the occupants from the stares of outsiders.

The shoulder strap of my seat belt presses uncomfortably against my neck.

At one time I knew these roads and the types of people who lived at the ends of these narrow driveways. I would have been able to enter their homes and sit at their Formica tables without feeling I was dressed in a uniform—today it's carefully pressed khakis and a designer polo shirt—that singled me out as a city girl.

Before I moved away I wouldn't have noticed the way women wore their pantyhose with the reinforced nylon toes poking through their open-toe shoes, or how they still grew and painted their fingernails so they resembled maroon claws. I've grown a habit of observing people in a clinical way that saddens me because it means I'm that much more alone, separate from these people I once knew.

God knows my parents deserve my attention, at least. Even now, when I've created a career and married a nice guy (a dentist, no less), there's something lacking between us. Something they can't place their finger on—*What is it with Zoe? Is it us?*

I imagine they sit around their kitchen nook discussing my absence. In my fictional scene they assume the best, as good people do. *Never mind.* My mother makes excuses as she wipes a drop of milk from the table—*She's so busy with her work. She has a husband. It's a long drive from the city.*

No doubt they look to the past to try to understand where things changed. But the past is like a wave that begins with an invisible wind ruffling the water's surface long before it crashes to shore. Even if I have regrets (and I have many), how is it possible to change what's already been stirred into motion? How could my parents, preoccupied by their own worries all these years, have even noticed the shift in the wind? Besides, the past is something I cannot speak about without betraying my sister.

Up ahead on the shoulder is a black lump. This stretch of highway, which runs through the Cree reservation, is rumoured to be the most dangerous in the province. Dilapidated houses line one side of the highway while a brand-new recreation centre towers incongruously on the other. It's a wealthy reservation compared to others because of its oil and gas rights, but there are still problems. The recent shooting of a toddler in drive-by gunfire made the national news. 'Isn't that close to where you grew up?' Calvin asked. 'Did you know any Indians personally?'

'That's just ten miles from Concord. And they're called First Nations now,' I corrected him.

Is the lump a darkly dressed body? A stray reservation dog felled by a pickup? I scold myself for seeing disaster in nothing. It's probably a garbage bag stuffed with trash: orange peels, coffee grounds, moldy bread ends. Or clothes that were headed for the Salvation Army second-hand store and fell off the back of a truck. The highway's centre rumble strip sends out a tremor beneath the car, warning me I'm getting too close to the middle of the road.

Calvin warned me to be careful on the highway: 'Turn back if it gets too much.' His brusque voice told me he was still upset from our horrible argument two nights ago, when we'd brushed up against matters best left alone.

'You're worried I'll put myself in danger on purpose?' I retorted.

He shrugged, which is what he usually did when he didn't know how to fix the conversation.

The only radio stations within range are evangelical talk shows or classic-rock programs. For nearly an hour I've listened to Reverend Tim on *The Prayer Hour*: 'God does not treat us as our sins deserve—man treats us as our sins deserve!'

Christ, enough of this. I turn the radio dial through high-pitched static, tuning in to the wail of Ozzy Osbourne's 'Crazy Train'.

At the last minute Calvin ran inside to get my multivitamins, which now rattle irritatingly on the empty passenger seat. 'Here,' he said breathlessly, 'don't forget to take these.' Even at his most annoyed, he was almost frustratingly considerate. His ability to see beyond his own emotions is what had attracted me in the first place. From the moment I met him I knew he would draw out the best in me, perhaps even cancel out my aloofness.

I reminded myself to thank him for the vitamins.

Why does his concern now provoke me? Am I tired of trying to be the right person for him? Has my comfortable life settled over me like a wool blanket, bulky and suffocating?

What I *did* know in the moment was this—life was stifling and I craved a respite. If I was looking for something more, I didn't know it yet.

Twice, he asked before I left, 'You're coming back Sunday?' He ran his fingers through his hair distractedly so he looked like a hedgehog. He paused as though he had something more to say.

'It's not like I want to stay there forever,' I replied quickly, not giving him a chance to talk. I resisted the urge to smooth his hair. Was he worried about the road conditions, or the way I'd complain about my family when I returned to Calgary—*I take time away from work, I drive all the way up there on my own, and for what? To feel like a stranger?* Was he worried I wasn't coming back?

Mostly I sensed he was glad that I'd be away from him for a while. For weeks we'd been tiptoeing around each other with the awkward politeness of a couple that has suddenly found itself in a predicament—keeping our topics neutral since any conversation that veered toward 'our situation' might erupt in cruel words.

A break will be good for both of us.

My parents will be pleased to see me, grateful for help with their packing. I am, after all, a professional organizer. I make a very good living, designing custom closets that end up photographed for decorating magazines—impressive shots of men's shirts hanging in tidy rows on chrome hangers, polished shoes peeking out from cognac-stained shelves. In my trunk is my box of supplies—a tape gun, a label maker, sheets of packing tissue, black Sharpie pens. Often Calvin teases me about my need for order: *Seriously, how many wicker baskets do we really need?*

My smallest travel bag sits on the passenger-side floor mat. I've packed few clothes, mainly yoga pants and T-shirts. For most of the week I'll be bending to fill boxes and driving my family crazy with my packing acronym, PURGE. *Pack. Use. Recycle. Give away. Eliminate.*

I've included my best jeans and a blow-dryer in case I need to get away from my mother, who's become a pack rat in her old age, refusing to part with things most people find useless—mismatched Tupperware, scraps of tinfoil, reused yogurt containers she fills with leftovers that go uneaten. *Honestly, Mom,* I can already hear myself saying, *you've got to let some of this stuff go.* If it gets to be too much I can always call Marnie, who'll be up for any kind of fun.

The last time I saw my parents was at Christmas, three months ago, when Calvin and I stopped for a visit on our way to Jasper National Park. We'd stayed only two hours, drinking coffee and eating shortbread from the dish my mother had set out as though we were guests. 'We should really get on the road,' I said, relieved to see snowflakes striking the window. My mother nodded wistfully while Dorothea stood up, eager to be rid of us. 'We booked the hotel weeks ago,' I reminded my mother. 'I invited you all to join us.'

'You know your father doesn't like to travel in the winter.'

I take a sip of peppermint tea from my Thermos. Is it my imagination or did the black lump shift closer onto the road?

I place the Thermos back in the cup holder and tighten my hands on the steering wheel. The cars behind me are coming up quickly; it would be foolish to slow down in these conditions. The cars ahead are disappearing one by one around a bend so it appears they're entering a black hole.

Before I know it, the car is alongside the dark lump, and I take my eyes off the road for a quick glance. I see, now, that it's just an empty black garbage bag, the sort of harmless piece of plastic that litters the side of any highway. But without warning, the bag flies up and into my windshield, blacking out my view. The interior of the car darkens with shadow. My foot taps the brake instinctively while my brain shoots out fragments of advice—*Don't hit the brakes or you'll skid!*

The bag tumbles up over the roof and onto the road behind me, dancing dangerously between cars. My own car wobbles, skating recklessly on the slippery road and over the rumble strip into the opposite lane. A truck moving toward me closes in alarmingly fast, its horn bleating a warning. Trees and hydro poles whip past, tall dark smudges on the landscape. My body goes numb.

God, please please please!

It feels as though it's minutes, but in seconds, my car catches the pavement again. Instinct takes over. I wrench the steering wheel to swerve back into my own lane as the truck whizzes past with only feet to spare. I keep my shaking foot on the gas pedal and glance in the rear-view mirror as the car behind mine slows.

Thank you, God.

The feeling in my body comes back in patches. First my legs, then my arms, even my cheeks prick back to life. As quickly as it veered out of control, my car is right again—one more vehicle on the assembly line of orderly traffic. My hands tremble but stay steady on the wheel.

By the time I get to my parents' house I'll be a wreck. They'll raise their eyebrows when I retell the near accident. My father will scold me in his pessimistic way—*You need to be more careful.*

Whenever he reminds me of my shortcomings I fight the urge to blurt out that he doesn't know the half of it. Of my greatest failing—of the tragedy I caused—he doesn't have a clue.

I stare at the road, already tired by the promise of a difficult week ahead. When I left Concord twenty years ago, in 1985, it was to make a new start, but there's that old ache in my belly of nostalgia and regret.

When I allow myself to remember the past, it's with great caution. A moment of indulgence that fools me into thinking that the worst hasn't yet happened—that if I'm careful, it may not happen. That the two of us, Dorothea and I, are still carefree young girls who lie sprawled on the rumpus room floor Friday evenings watching *Fantasy Island* with the teak bowl of Jiffy Pop between us, our fingers not yet shrinking back from an accidental touch.

It was there, in the rumpus room, that our father, in his better moods,

played airplane—lying on his back and placing his raised feet in the softness of our bellies while we soared above him screeching with delight. We
were too big for this game but that didn't stop him from poking his head
through the beaded-curtain door to ask in his oddly accented voice, 'Who
first?'

'Me! Me!' we cried, scrambling for the chance to spread our arms out
like wings. 'Don't drop me,' we shrieked, feeling our thin, preteen bodies
tilting toward the carpet.

'You can't get hurt,' he said, wincing at the weight of us. 'I promise
you.'

These are the moments to remember—the times when we could still
sit together on the sofa without shifting away from each other to avoid
contact. When pauses in conversations didn't threaten like storm clouds.
When we could place our bodies in someone else's hands and let go, sus-
pended in the air with ease, knowing that if we slipped someone would
cushion our fall.

These moments are the better part of my memory, the bittersweet
recollection of a time before we even understood we could fall—or how
brutally that fall would tear us apart.

Two

'You didn't need to come,' my mother says, standing with her arms crossed over her chest. 'I can manage on my own.'

'I know you can manage,' I reply, aware that I'm holding my travel bag between us like a shield. 'But I do this sort of thing for a living. I thought you'd be glad to see me.'

Dorothea stands at the top of the stairs looking down at us. 'Did you remember to bring the tape gun?'

Already I'm irritated and it hasn't even been five minutes.

'That Zoe?' my father yells from the kitchen.

'Who else would it be?' my mother yells back. She motions for Dorothea and me to come to the kitchen as though we are children. She tells me, 'Of course I'm glad to see you. It would be nice to see you more often.'

I feel myself tightening at the shoulders.

My father and my nephew, Ryan, wait at the table. I smile at Ryan, who hides behind his Spider-Man comic book. 'Hello, Auntie.' He smiles shyly from behind his book, revealing only a trace of the scar from his most recent cleft-palate surgery.

'Hello, monster. Good book?'

'It's okay.'

'You're reading a lot these days?'

He shrugs and puts the comic down. 'You sit here. Beside me.'

I sit down and smile at my father. 'You're doing all right, Dad?'

Ryan touches my arm. 'He doesn't hear very well.'

'I know, sweetie.' I touch his hand, surprised by how easily he takes it. I haven't spent much time with Ryan since I lived in Edmonton and helped care for him on the rare weekends I came home to Concord. Dorothea had moved back into my parents' home when she'd had Ryan, at first refusing my mother's offer but quickly realizing how difficult it was on her own. I'd learned how to feed Ryan with an eye dropper from my mother, who was convinced Dorothea's *lifestyle* had caused the injury to his lip. I'd held Ryan's sleeping body wrapped in a soft cotton blanket and hoped my parents would overcome their disappointment that Dorothea had gotten herself pregnant without finishing her education. My mother's bridge club friends, no doubt relieved it wasn't their own daughter, had assured her, *There are thousands of single parents out there. She'll be fine.*

A part of me had been glad to no longer be the focus of my parents' criticisms—when was I going to use my teaching degree? Did I really plan to clean closets for the rest of my life?

My father asks, 'The roads were okay?'

'Fine,' I lie.

'You must be hungry. Sit down.' My mother ties on an apron.

'Give the girl a chance to get settled.'

'Nonsense. She's come all this way. She must be starving.' My mother has put out her best china service and rolled paper serviettes into festive cones. She has gone to the effort of making cheese-filled *tyropita* from the Greek cookbook my father brought back from one of his trips home to Athens. My mother, who is from a nearby Alberta farming community, is most used to frying pork chops and boiling asparagus until it is bitter grey mush.

'You must've been cooking all day.' I unravel my cone and place it on my lap. 'This looks great.'

'It's nothing.' My mother waves her hand but looks pleased.

'I was surprised to hear you'd convinced Dad to move to a seniors' home.'

She sits at the table and sighs. 'It's not a seniors' home. They're adult apartments. You remember George and Celia Warren? They moved in last year; they've been so busy we hardly see them anymore. They've already been to the casino in Regina by bus. In May they're going for their second wine tour of the Okanagan. They say it's just like visiting the California wineries, only cheaper.'

'Dad's going to be okay living with other people?'

'You know how Greeks like to bellyache. Your father will be fine once we get settled in the new apartment. We can't stay in this house forever, especially now that Dorothea and Ryan are moving out.' She passes a bowl of potatoes to my father.

'You shouldn't talk about Dad like he isn't sitting here.' Dorothea crumples her napkin into a ball.

'Now you're telling me how to have a proper conversation?' Immediately I regret my tone.

'Girls,' my mother warns, rubbing her temples.

My father points his knife at Ryan, who pushes peas one at a time into his mouth. 'The boy should keep his mouth closed when he chews. His fingers are filthy.'

'He's only eight.' Dorothea reaches over and picks up a couple of loose peas. She snatches away Ryan's drinking glass as his elbow nearly tips it over. 'I told you, watch your milk!'

At the end of the week the moving truck will come to pick up my parents' belongings. Then I can repack my small bag to go back to Calgary, where I spend weekdays installing step shelves in clients' pantries to display their canned food in stadium-seating order, or ruthlessly weeding their closets of scuffed shoes and pilled sweaters. The things people hang on to, I'll never understand.

I help myself to the mashed potatoes served in the blue glass bowl that's been in our family for as long as I can remember. Along with the potatoes, there are opaque slices of cucumber drowning in syrupy dill vinaigrette, and string beans mixed with Campbell's mushroom soup and slivered almonds. There's a current trend in Calgary restaurants toward *gourmet comfort food*. Organic turkey chili, wild mushroom perogy—the kind of food that makes my father, who owned the Parthenon Pizza and Steak House for twenty-two years, roll his eyes. *Give me a T-bone steak any day*, he's fond of saying. *And don't charge me a fortune!*

'So,' I ask Dorothea in a friendlier tone, 'is your new place near the community college?'

'Yup.' She turns the plastic margarine tub around to read the fine print, stabbing its smooth yellow surface with her knife.

Although we grew up together, at times sharing a bed to wake up to each other's warm, damp breath in our ear, we now barely speak. Dorothea calls only to report bad news.

In case you care, Dad's been to see the specialist about his heart.

Mom's getting cataract surgery.

And last month: *If you haven't heard yet, Mom and Dad are moving to a seniors' home.*

I remind myself to stay in the present.

'When are you moving out?' I ask Dorothea.

'I've already moved most of my boxes. I'll stay here until Mom and Dad are packed up. I'll be gone by Sunday.'

'I'll give you a hand.'

'I'll be fine by myself.'

'I'm sure Ryan would like to show me his new bedroom.' I smile at Ryan.

He smiles back. 'I got a new bunk bed.'

I tease, 'A bunk bed? Are you old enough for a bunk bed?' I'm at my easiest with Ryan. The feelings I have for my sister—the feelings of affection I don't know what to do with—get directed toward Ryan in the way of expensive presents and generous birthday cheques sent through the mail and that my sister calls to thank me for grudgingly. In a recent call she'd been curt, 'We don't need charity.'

'It's hardly charity,' I replied, ignoring the thought of blood money. 'It's for Ryan. For his new bedroom, or whatever you'd like to do with it.' If I'd hoped she'd see that my intentions were good, I was mistaken.

'Your sister's doing very well in college.' My father tears the middle from a slice of bread with trembling fingers. 'She should finally be able to support herself.'

I know that even if Dorothea doesn't see it, my father is offering a compliment. It's his style to temper approval with gruffness. When I brought Calvin home for the first time, my parents were pleased. 'A dentist!' my mother had exclaimed, serving him Labatt's in her best crystal glass. 'You won't find better.' She jabbed me playfully in the arm when he got up to use the washroom. But my father couldn't help being cynical. 'Who knows ... maybe he isn't ready to be serious.'

I'd met Calvin at a New Year's party, shortly after I'd moved from Edmonton to Calgary.

'So you're a teacher?' Calvin had asked, shouting over the music.

'I used to be,' I shouted back, and then corrected myself after seeing the puzzled expression on his face. 'I mean, I still am. It's not like I lost my teaching certificate or anything like that.' After high school, I'd moved to Edmonton to take elementary-education courses at the University of Alberta on a scholarship because that's what my parents wanted, and there was nothing else that interested me enough for me to protest against the idea. My father had been practical—*There's always a need for teachers, even in a bad economy. You'll have long vacations, a good pension.* But my student teaching practicum was enough to convince me I wouldn't enjoy being responsible for the gremlin-faced children who tugged at my sleeves. To the dismay of my parents I'd worked as a manager of a California Closets franchise for nearly ten years before I moved to Calgary, never once using my teaching certificate.

'Don't worry,' Calvin said. 'I rarely assume the worst.'

I was relieved to witness his easygoing personality, so different from my own.

After the New Year's party Calvin and I found ourselves in a warm Chinatown restaurant pulling apart barbecue duck with our fingers. Flakes of snow formed a shawl of lace on the ground outside, giving me a sense of lightheartedness I hadn't felt in months. Six months later, when I suspected Calvin was about to propose during dinner at Big Fish Sushi, I became anxious and turned away to peer at the lethargic fish circling the restaurant's cloudy aquarium. Calvin used the fat end of his chopstick to turn my head gently back toward him: 'You know this is right.'

I nodded, unable to speak. But even as he said the words—*marry me*—and I replied—*okay*—a part of me doubted, because he had not yet witnessed the restless gale that whirled inside me, causing me to act, at times, on what I knew was my destructive nature. If I tried to explain he would have shushed me, telling me I was being too hard on myself. Perhaps he was right—it had been a long time since I'd let anyone down. And so I ignored my misgivings.

Dorothea pushes the lid onto the margarine container. 'Time for your bath,' she says to Ryan, who is wiping his mouth with his sleeve. She avoids our eyes, clearly annoyed with the conversation, as she guides Ryan toward the bathroom.

My father looks at me. 'Tell me—what did I say wrong?'

'Forget it.' I know the best thing to do is ignore his question.

'She's always so angry, that kid.'

The issue of my sister's temper has been an ongoing topic of discussion since she was a teenager. After I left home for university in Edmonton, I thought I'd escaped the situation. But I was still bothered by the long-distance phone calls from my distraught mother—*Your sister didn't even come home last night.* Being eighteen, it was easy for me to push away the thought of fifteen-year-old Dorothea drifting in and out of the Night Owl Arcade with the other darkly dressed misfits who just a few years earlier we'd crossed the street to avoid.

I knew if I came home I'd be pestered by my parents to rescue my sister. In the past, I'd found drug paraphernalia—blackened pipes, rolling papers—in the bottom drawer of her bureau under a heap of sweatshirts. *Her self-esteem is so low,* my mother lamented. *She's a pretty girl, even with the ear. I wish she didn't try so hard for attention from boys.* Although she didn't mean to, my mother always made me feel responsible.

There had been frequent battles between my parents and my sister over homework and friends throughout high school. She'd made a half-hearted attempt at university that ended after a few months when she moved in with a boyfriend in Edmonton's gritty north downtown. By then I was working at California Closets in a bright shiny strip mall in the industrial end of the city. My apartment was small but clean, and close to a bus stop.

One afternoon she showed up at the mall wet and shivering from a rainstorm. Judging by her red-rimmed eyes she'd been crying and was clearly high, talking about the boyfriend, Mason, who'd been busted for selling pot—*I can't go back right now.*

I bought her a cup of coffee and a cinnamon roll at the nearby Tim Hortons and told her to wait for my shift to end. Afterwards I took her home on the bus, avoiding the eyes of people who took one look at her stringy hair and shabby boots, and looked away. She'd stared out the window as we drove through the suburbs, picking at her frayed jacket collar and not saying a word. I got her dry sweatpants and a heavy sweatshirt, making a bed for her on the sofa. She pushed away the toast and jam I'd made, and wiped her eyes, teary and bleeding with mascara, on the blanket. 'I'm such a fuck-up.'

'Don't say that.' I sat on the floor uncomfortably. 'You'll figure it out.'

'It's not just Mason, it's my whole life.'

'You can go back to school. You're so young.'

She snorted.

'Just lie down. Everything will look better in the morning.' I was speaking in platitudes, not sure anything would look better in the morning. My parents had been worrying for years that she'd end up as one of those drifters who never seemed to settle into anything—or any-one—worthwhile. They had no idea why she'd drifted off the course of her life, and I was too cowardly to confess the reason. All I could do was take over for the moment, pulling the blanket over her impossibly thin body that wore my freshly laundered clothes, which I'd chosen carefully thinking they might be the last decent ones she'd wear for a while.

She put her head down obediently, falling asleep quickly. I stayed on the floor, inches from her pretty face, noticing how her unwashed hair was still thick and auburn. Her lips were pink as a child's, the pigments of her skin and hair bravely holding up to the rigours of too little food and sleep.

In the morning she was gone, my clothes folded in a neat pile on the sofa beside the blanket that held the stain of her tears. For nearly a decade afterwards, she lived at the margins of our lives, working at a string of late-night diners and calling my parents only when she needed money to cover the rent. When she moved back to Concord with three-month-old Ryan to live with my parents, she brought her sour temper with her. When I made the move farther away to Calgary to work for a prominent interior design firm six years ago, I told my parents it was for the salary. The truth was, I'd grown tired of thinking of excuses not to spend weekends in Concord, where the fog of my sister's sulkiness hung in the air.

Now, in the kitchen with my father, I know I should defend Dorothea. There are things he doesn't know, or understand, about her tendency to retreat. If I try to explain that she's protecting herself, he'll furrow his eyebrows and ask, *Why?* How can I explain that she has secrets she doesn't want to reveal? That she's protecting not only herself, but me?

I've lost the right to defend my sister. If I stand up for Dorothea now she'll feel I'm interfering. It's been many years since I tried to protect my little sister.

The incident with her ear plainly stands out—

I was fifteen, and Dorothea twelve, when the wooden corner of my swing struck her in the ear during summer camp. Before the incident I'd been caught up in my thoughts, angry at having to take my sister—who was prone to fits of homesickness—to day camp instead of joining my friends who'd invited me to their cabins at nearby Bitter Lake. I barely noticed the *vroom* of whizzing cars or a camp leader's occasional scolding of a child for getting too close to the busy road. Before Dorothea's body fell motionless at my feet, I was daydreaming about Bitter Lake, where my friends were spending their summer days: The snapping of soda-can tabs. The hissing and popping of steak fat on the barbecue grill. The fizzle of rye and Coke poured over cracking ice by men who, unlike my father, dressed in denim cut-offs and sprawled good-naturedly on lounge chairs.

My friend Kara Gunnerson's parents owned a waterfront cabin with an indoor bathroom. Though I'd only been out to Bitter Lake once that year, in my mind's eye I could touch the almost white fuzz of Kara's arms bleached by the sun. Her skin was malted-milk brown from Hawaiian

Tropic tanning oil and days spent lying outdoors on a soft velour aqua beach towel—unlike the coarse, overwashed beach towels of my own house. Her pale blond hair falling over her shoulders, squinting from the sun with her usual look of annoyance, Kara would be propped up on her elbows reading adult romances pilfered from her parents' bedroom.

Because of Dorothea, I was stuck in town making shell-pasta necklaces and tiptoeing across the clammy concrete floor at the outdoor pool with elementary school children, aware that Kara and my other friends were digging their toes into the warm sand of Bitter Lake's beach. When they reminisced about their summer vacation it seemed they were also reminding me that they were growing up, and moving beyond my reach. *Oh, that's right.* They would titter when I stared at them blankly—*You weren't there.*

I was saddled, then, with my little sister, wishing life would offer a diversion from my boredom. So when Dorothea ran in front of my swing I didn't dig my heels in the dirt to prevent the blow.

At first the camp leaders were too stunned by the blood to move. Then time sped ahead and everything happened at once. One of the leaders ran across the street to the pay phone; another placed swim towels under Dorothea's head. The ambulance and my mother's car pulled up to the curb at the same time. The blood from Dorothea's ear soaked through the towels into the dust. My mother shoved through the circle of kids swarming around the swing set. The youngest kids sat quietly on the merry-go-round—for the first time all summer they didn't need to be reminded to *quiet down!*

I sat on the curb hugging my knees to my chest and watched my mother climb into the ambulance. The flashing red lights cast a wide circle, staining my forearms red.

'It was an accident,' the adults said, turning their serious eyes to me. 'Don't feel bad.' But I knew better. And the worst part was I couldn't help but hope my mother would find the camp program too dangerous, and I would finally be allowed to spend the summer with Kara and the other girls at Bitter Lake. *You should've watched where you were going,* my mother had chided Dorothea afterwards, pulling her close at the same time.

I hear Ryan splashing in the bath. I stare at the lone string bean on my plate; it curls into itself like a snake. 'You should be easier on Dorothea,' I say to my father. 'She's doing a fine job.'

'Hearing aid's on the fritz,' my mother shouts. 'He can't hear you.'

He jerks his head. 'I can hear what you're all saying about me!'

'Good for you.' She gets up and busies herself stacking clean Yoplait containers from the dishwasher. A plastic lid slips from her hand and she reaches for it, stumbling to the floor.

'Mom!' I bolt from my seat. 'Are you all right?'

Flustered, she pushes me away. 'Don't be ridiculous. It's just my knees.'

'What's wrong with your knees?' The guilt again, telling me I haven't been around enough to know her knees have become a problem.

My father answers for her. 'The knees are giving out. Doctor says they might need to be replaced.'

'Why didn't anyone tell me?'

My mother is annoyed by the attention. 'Will everyone quit fussing over my knees? You'd think I was dying.'

'Why don't you let me empty the dishwasher?' I take her by the hand.

'Honestly, Zoe.' She brushes my hand away. 'I've been getting by just fine on my own, thank you very much.'

'Well, Mom, I'm here to help. I *want* to help.'

She softens and puts a hand to my head, pushing away a stray hair. 'I know you do, honey. I don't mean to hurt your feelings. But please don't fret over me.'

I'm overtaken by the urge to crumple into her arms. How long has it been since anyone touched me like this? Calvin's affection always has a sexual motive. His hand may start at my hair but it inevitably reaches my waist or my breasts.

My mother moves back to the dishwasher and the moment is over.

Her voice takes on a brisk tone, telling me she's embarrassed at having shown her emotion: 'Have you called Calvin yet?'

'I'll call after dinner.'

'I suppose you'll be calling that Marnie tonight, too.'

'What's the big deal if I call Marnie?'

'I don't know.' Her mouth tightens. 'The last time you stayed here overnight you were out with Marnie until two-thirty in the morning.' She places two blue pills in my palm. 'Here, give these to your father.' She sits heavily on a stool. 'Marnie wasn't all that nice to you when you were growing up. You forget how many times she let you down.'

My palm grows damp. 'That was a long time ago, people change. Besides, she can be good fun.' Marnie and I have little in common other than shared experiences from long ago. But old friends are similar to family. Something draws you in year after year—a hopeful but maddening tendency to think that *this time* things might be different. Friends from the past are similar to items in a closet that you can't imagine throwing away. Even it if doesn't fit, or is fraying at the edge, you hang on to the item because you know you'll never be able to replace it. It reminds you of an occasion, or a time, you wish to remember—even if you can't say why, exactly.

My mother shrugs. 'If you say so.'

I follow my father as he shuffles toward the living room. He seems to have grown smaller, his frame hunching forward with age. My chest tightens. Why haven't I noticed until now? He sits heavily in his La-Z-Boy recliner and picks the pills from my hand. 'You're going to help your mother with the movers, right?'

'That's why I'm here, isn't it?' I say, ignoring the fact that I'm dying to contact Kyle Lipinski, too. A month ago I'd impulsively looked Kyle up on Classmates.com, sending him a note before I had time to reconsider:

Hi there.

I hope you don't mind receiving this letter but I think of you often and hope you're doing well. Write back if you feel like it.

Yours, Zoe Lemonopolous

It had been a long time since I'd done anything so reckless. With my parents' impending move to the Vista Grande, my pull to Concord (and the past) had become greater than usual. Possibly I was looking for a conclusion to the awful circumstance that had irrevocably split Kyle and me apart. Was there anything he could say that would lessen the damage we'd caused? Or did I merely want to share the guilty load I still carried?

Perhaps, also, I was looking for a diversion from my growing annoyance with Calvin, who was trying too hard to make everything right in our current situation. Or rather, trying to make everything right about *me*.

Perhaps it was for all these reasons. All I knew was, the present seemed heavy, and I needed something else to occupy my thoughts. It was as though my mind had scanned its past for the one person who could match my restlessness.

Compulsively I'd checked my computer until a reply came from Kyle two days later. *It was great hearing from you,* he wrote. *I think of you often, too.*

The last time I'd seen him was the autumn following high school. We met by chance on a corner of Main Street, he heading in one direction, I in the other. 'I've been meaning to call ...' he said, too uncomfortable to meet my eyes. When the light turned green he stepped onto the street. 'I should get back to work.'

I nodded, resisting the urge to grab him by the arm so we could talk about what had happened with Dorothea that August. But then he was gone, his back moving away from me as he crossed Main Street.

Over the years Marnie has talked about them all—Kyle, Kara, Janice, even Cam, whose disappearance caused no end of speculation, and whom I was most afraid to discuss—as though speaking his name might make him reappear. But the one who pulled at me most was Kyle.

From what Marnie has told me, he and Kara Gunnerson have a ten-year-old daughter who lives with him full-time. He makes his living as a cabinetmaker, but works as an artist as well, creating panel paintings made of gesso and linen based on a centuries-old technique. His panels depict disturbing scenes of prairie life with religious undertones, and are beginning to earn him a reputation. A recent article in the *Calgary Herald* ran beneath the headline, 'Prairie Artist Tackles Modern Themes in a Decidedly Unmodern Way'.

My father settles deeper into his recliner and washes the pills down with coffee. I tuck a pillow beneath his head. He looks up, surprised.

'What's wrong?' I ask.

'Nothing, *koukla mou.*' He smiles, pleased with the pillow.

I busy myself by pushing the coffee table closer to his chair, suddenly shy about his use of a Greek endearment from long ago—*my little doll.* How had I forgotten the childhood name he'd given me, more familiar when I was young than my own name? This was what I dreaded most about coming home, these nostalgic moments that open me up like a wound.

Very soon I will pack the last of this room away—the throw cushions strategically placed to hide nail polish stains. The Hudson's Bay wool blanket shaggy from years of use. The embroidered deer-head coasters that sit neatly stacked atop the coffee table beside the pile of *Reader's Digests* my father refuses to throw out.

Over half of my life has been lived away from this house. As a teenager

I spent long afternoons lying on my single bed with its white fringed blanket, tearing the fringes apart as I contemplated what now seem clearly to have been silly teenage grievances. If I thought of my family at all back then it was with a grudging tolerance. My father's mispronounced English was an embarrassment. My sister's whining presence had been as annoying as a pebble in my shoe. Is there anything as self-absorbed as a teenage girl?

After my parents go to bed and the house has been quiet for at least a half hour, I push the garage door open and sit on the cold concrete steps, shivering from the chill through my thin yoga pants. I light a cigarette, knowing that my mother would be distressed to know I'm still smoking. I will try hard to please her in other ways. I will not phone Marnie; that will please my mother greatly. And I will not contact Kyle no matter how much I want to.

Who am I kidding?

Three

After Kyle's first e-mail he'd contacted me again to invite me to a showing of his panel paintings at the contemporary Truck Gallery in Calgary. *It's not your typical art show,* he wrote, *but you're welcome to come and see for yourself.*

I mentioned it casually to Calvin. 'A friend—an old boyfriend, really—has a showing at the Truck Gallery this weekend. What do you think about going?'

'What's the subject matter?'

I'd looked it up online, disappointed that there was no photo to accompany Kyle's biography. The title of the show was *A Terrible Romance: New Works by Modern Prairie Gothic Artists.*

'You should go,' Calvin said, after seeing the online gallery. 'Take Frances, she'll enjoy it.'

'You think?'

'Well, it's not my sort of thing, is it?'

'Not really.'

I'd been both relieved and anxious he hadn't wanted to come.

Frances, my only real girlfriend, had jumped at the chance. When we got to the gallery, she looked around eagerly. 'Do you see him yet? Why do you think he invited you?'

I shrugged. How would I know anymore what was in Kyle's mind?

Then I saw him, talking to a woman in tortoiseshell-rimmed eyeglasses and tweed culottes. My own jersey skirt clung to my hips, too tightly I realized.

How could I have thought the sight of him would have little effect, that his sandy hair growing a shade too long so it hit the collar at the back of his shirt, wouldn't make me gasp in recognition?

'Jesus,' said Frances, who was prone to speaking her mind. 'You've still got it bad.'

'Don't be ridiculous,' I replied. 'He's not my type anymore.'

'Right.' She smirked, poking me in the side with her finger in her overly confident manner. It was what I liked most about Frances, her assurance that she would be *liked.* She was one of the few people who could make me laugh so hard I barely recognized myself.

Kyle seemed to sense me then, his head cocking, then his face and body turning slowly until he was facing me. I resisted the urge to tug my skirt into submission.

'Hey.' He took a step toward me.

'Hey yourself.'

I stepped into his arms for an uneasy hug.

'I'll be back, don't worry about me.' Frances disappeared into the washroom.

'I've scared your friend away,' he said, stepping back. 'But it's great to see you, come and look around.' He took me by the waist without waiting for an answer, guiding me toward his delicate panels. Here was a work entitled *Female Gothic*, a woman running away from a farmhouse in daytime, wearing a tattered shirt-dress, the shadow of the farmhouse appearing as a medieval arch looming menacingly over the woman and clothes drying on a line.

'What does it mean?' I asked cautiously.

'I'm trying to create a sense of irony. The idea of modern hell, found in an everyday setting. I rejected the darkness of a traditional panel to show how horror seems worse in daylight. You know, for all our so-called enlightenment, we haven't really changed. So I guess this painting is about the unchanging nature of mankind. Or rather, womankind.' He laughed. 'God, I sound pretentious.'

'Not at all.' I was beyond intrigued, but also worried—I'd hoped he wouldn't be so refined, that we would have grown impossibly apart. His hand still lay on my waist possessively.

He cleared his throat self-consciously. 'I'm trying to be sincere, not campy.'

'And this one?' I pointed to *Harvest Time*, an enormous panel of crows sitting on an electrical line high above a downtown setting while workers in business suits rushed in and out of office towers far below the sinister watch of the birds.

'I thought of the nature of crows—of what a nuisance they are to farmers while in the city they go unnoticed. And how the crows want to keep their power even in the face of invisibility.'

'I like how you've given it all so much thought. But this one'—I pointed to a series of panels entitled *The Coming Terror*— 'it's realistic for sure, but so heavy.' There were three arched panels linked together to create a series of home life: the first panel a scene of a couple eating, bored, in front of the television; the second a scene of the woman looking out a window at a church spire while the husband napped on the sofa; the final panel showing a Christ-like infant gilded with gold leaf, lying neglected and forgotten in the middle of the floor.

'I'm not sure I can articulate that one, it's expressive more than anything. An extension of my mood at the time.'

'So you don't know what it means?'

He grinned. 'I forgot how serious you can be.'

'I'm not serious,' I protested, then laughed at myself. 'Maybe a little.'

We sat down on a viewing bench across from a painting by a different artist, a mixed-media expression of a genderless red-cloaked figure wandering lost and ghostlike into a swirling river, the type of painting my father would scoff at and call *a waste of paint*. The solitary figure made me think of Dorothea with a sadness that came like a sudden kick to the stomach.

'It seems unreal that you're here,' Kyle said.

'I know.' My insides roiled as the river did, chaotic and excited at the same time. I hadn't known what to expect—in the past Kyle had often been closed. Now he seemed reachable, as though the art show was merely a backdrop for our meeting. The high ceilings appeared to go on forever, as though anything were possible within these walls. The surroundings made me bold. 'I wanted to see you. To see how you'd ... I don't know—'

'Turned out?'

'No, not exactly. To be so close to someone and then never see them again. It would be sad, don't you think?' I looked down when I said it, not sure what his reaction would be. My hands trembled in my lap. Here we were, twenty years later, and I still came unhinged. I braced my arms on the bench to steady myself.

He placed his hand beside mine so they were nearly touching. 'I'm glad you came. I was hoping things were okay between us.'

I nodded, barely able to breathe from the closeness of him. 'Mostly.' A pause. 'We've never really talked since that final summer.' A small, apologetic laugh. 'But mostly, I guess.'

'Let's not talk about that now.' His hand moved to touch mine, so slightly I might have thought it was a mistake if I didn't know him better. But his attempt to silence the past made me uneasy.

The woman in the culottes returned and hovered as though to remind him he needed to get back to business. He stood up reluctantly.

'I should let you go.' I waved him on. 'You've got other people to talk to.'

'You okay?' His eyes searched mine. Surely the magnet of our attraction would have grown weaker by now.

I wasn't okay. I had so many questions.

The woman smiled at us both, impatient. He mouthed, *Goodbye*, and grinned before turning away.

Taking Frances home, I had difficulty driving. My mind, preoccupied with the touch of his fingers, couldn't keep the gas and brake pedals straight. How could desire for and disappointment in a person exist at the same time?

We drove toward the main street of Inglewood, whose turn-of-the-century buildings housed cafés, antique stores and small clothing boutiques. I made the wrong turn at the edge of downtown which took us past the seedy Cecil Hotel.

'Are you all right?' Frances asked. 'You should have gone the other way.'

'Yes, of course.'

'You think I can't see what's written on your face?'

I worried—would Calvin see the same thing? But when I walked through the front door he barely looked up from his hockey game. I could tell by the bowl of nachos and empty beer bottle that he'd enjoyed himself without me. He asked, 'How was the art show?'

'Fine.' I threw my keys distractedly on the foyer table, missing the basket.

'Can you make a living from that sort of thing?'

'I don't know.' I picked up the keys and dropped them in their proper place. 'What does that matter?'

'You were gone a long time.'

'What's that supposed to mean?'

'Nothing. I was starting to get concerned.'

'He's just an old boyfriend from a million years ago. Surely you're not jealous?'

'No. But I think you should be taking better care of yourself. You've been on the go since this morning.'

'You're being ridiculous.' But he was right to be concerned. I'd barely sat down all day. I had even absent-mindedly taken a sip of Frances's wine.

Why was it that I forgot everything else when I was with Kyle? Hadn't we learned our lesson?

I've replayed that evening in my mind more times than I care to admit. I know I shouldn't contact Kyle while I'm here in Concord. I have come, in part, to tell my parents The Big News. For weeks Calvin and I have been getting used to the idea ourselves. When I told Calvin I'd accidentally become pregnant he seemed relieved that the decision had been made for us. 'I guess it was meant to be, then.' He'd placed his hand on my abdomen.

'I guess so.'

He withdrew his hand, seeing the doubt in my face. 'You're not even a little bit happy?' His face gave away his disappointment.

And there it was—the chink in our dam.

The discord that won't go away.

I sit, now, in my parents' garage, grinding out my nearly whole cigarette. I've justified the occasional puff but my destructive habits need to stop. I wrap my arms protectively around my belly as I've seen other women do. By now I'd expected to feel excitement instead of this persistent unease.

Four

The week before I took the pregnancy test, Calvin brought up the subject of babies. Or rather, he talked about the way I'd *looked* at the baby that bobbed past us in Safeway in a navy chest harness drooling onto its mother's jacket, while we picked through tomatoes looking for ones without bruises.

'What was that all about?' Calvin broached the subject when we were home in our kitchen unpacking the groceries. He placed the lemongrass stalks and parsley bundles in the vegetable crisper, the low-sodium soy sauce in the refrigerator's side door and the whole-grain bagels in the breadbasket. He checked the pot in which his Gouda was melting for cheese fondue. We were having guests for dinner.

'What do you mean?' *Christ*, I thought, *we're talking about this again*. For days I'd been looking nervously for signs of my period, going to the bathroom every few hours. Even though we'd had several conversations about getting pregnant I never considered it might happen by accident. At thirty-eight years old it was supposed to be difficult to get pregnant.

'The baby. Why did you look at the baby that way?' He whisked fiercely.

I wound a plastic Safeway bag around my fingers until they turned white. 'What's with you and babies lately?'

'The way you looked at that baby. As though it were—I don't know. Some sort of monster.' He narrowed his eyes at the pot.

'I hardly looked at the child.' I crushed the plastic bag into a ball and tossed it in the recycling can, which was already full. It exasperated me that Calvin let the recycling and trash cans build up to the point of overflowing. What sort of additional burdens would I have with a baby? 'Anyway'—I took the spoon rest from its spot beside a heavy ceramic jar stuffed full of takeout chopsticks and handed it to him—'it's not as if you like children either.'

He grated more cheese into a bowl. 'Where'd you get the idea I dislike children?'

'Come on. You make fun of all our friends who have them. You're always saying how the mothers are fat and boring. And how much you hate the baby talk.'

'All that disgusting information about infected nipples and leaking breasts? *Stitches*?' He tilted a carton of cream into the bubbling pot. 'It doesn't mean I dislike children.'

'Speaking of kids—are Sasha and Michael bringing their precious bundle?' I knew I sounded bitchy.

He sprinkled pepper into the pot. 'They're bringing him, yes.'

'What's its name again?'

'Oscar. His name is Oscar.'

'What the hell kind of name is that? Do you know what it costs to raise a kid these days?'

'How would I know?'

'One hundred and sixty thousand dollars.'

'Where did you learn that? Does that include university?'

'The *Globe and Mail*. No university.'

He turned the stove dial to low. 'It might be nice when you're older to have children help care for you. Look how happy Sasha is. She didn't seem the type to want children either.'

The heat of the kitchen tired me almost as much as the conversation. I tore off a piece of bagel with my teeth. 'You have kids because you want to have kids. Not so you'll have someone to look after you when you're old. Anyway, Sasha's got no business having children, if you ask me.'

'You're talking about the affair?'

'It's over now. Maybe the baby will change things between her and Michael. But why are we talking about this again? It always ends in a fight.'

He leaned against the counter and thought for a minute. Then he rinsed the cheese grater and put it in the dishwasher. 'I guess we need to make a decision instead of running this argument around and around. You're not getting any younger.'

'I don't know what you want me to say.' I pulled a dime from the jar beside the telephone. 'Would you like to flip for it? We're not going to be able to make this decision on our own.'

'Don't be so cavalier.'

'No, really. We'll decide on a coin toss, it's easier than these endless discussions. Heads, yes baby. Tails, no baby.'

He placed an arm on my shoulder. 'C'mon.' His voice was strained. 'Don't be like this.'

I tossed the coin in the air. It landed heads-side up, making a dull sound against the cork floor we'd laid six months earlier because I'd

— 32 —

admired a photo in a decorating magazine. My bare feet looked thin and graceful next to his in their slouched athletic socks.

He squatted to pick up the coin. I stared at him for a long moment, unwilling to speak about it anymore. Then I looked at the clock and turned toward the hallway, weary with the expectation of our guests. My hands pressed against the curve of my abdomen—it was still flat. I was already three weeks late with my period; I'd never been late before. With my need to control everything I was sure I'd be an awful mother.

Later that evening, when Sasha and Michael were gone and we were getting ready for bed, Calvin asked, 'Why do you suppose she had the affair?'

'I think she just wanted a bit of excitement. You know, even though Michael's a terrific guy, he's a bit bland. Don't you think?'

'If by bland you mean dependable and decent. I guess that makes me a bit bland, too.'

'Oh God.' I rolled my eyes at him in the bathroom mirror and put down my toothbrush. 'Let's not make this about us.'

'I'm just saying it's a shitty thing.'

I turned off the bathroom light to signal the end of the conversation and walked to the bedroom. 'I agree.'

We lay in the dark for a few minutes. He sat up in bed. 'I know you'd tell me, if you felt that way.'

'That sounds more like a question.'

'Not really.' He touched my foot with his.

'Well, it does,' I said, unreasonably irked by his need for reassurance. 'Don't worry so much,' I said, resisting the urge to withdraw my foot from his. At the time, I meant it.

Five

A plastic Jesus dangles from the rear-view mirror of Kyle's truck. 'Omigod, I can't believe it!' I laugh and grab Jesus's small cold body.

Last night I sat in my parents' garage promising myself I wouldn't contact Marnie. But tonight she'd phoned me. 'You told me you'd call when you got here,' she scolded. 'I need to get away from my goddamn kids.'

Marnie and I had gone to Rattler's Lounge, where everyone over thirty went for drinks, two-stepping on the dance floor to Garth Brooks or the Dixie Chicks. Any night of the week Rattler's was packed with people dancing or playing billiards—many of them stumbling out to the parking lot after midnight telling themselves they were fine to drive home.

I e-mailed Kyle from the computer in my parents' basement before Marnie picked me up in a taxi. I told myself I was just being friendly, typing the words before I could change my mind: *Guess who's in town? Rattler's tonight?*

He wrote back: *I'll be there. Wait for me.*

Ever since the art show we'd been exchanging e-mails. I hadn't expected he'd be much of a writer, but his last letter had surprised me with its openness:

I have to admit I was hoping you'd come to the gallery show. I can't believe how little you've changed. I keep thinking about that night, and hope we can stay in touch. I hope it's all right to say that.

'Do you think he'll show up?' Marnie sucked her strawberry daiquiri through a straw. The tables in Rattler's were made of old recycled wagon wheels topped with glass that was sticky with beer rings.

'Who knows?' I popped a salted peanut into my mouth. At my favourite Calgary lounge they always served Japanese wasabi-flavoured rice crackers. Frances would have a laugh about the drink specials here—two-for-one shooters with names like Prairie Oyster and Sex on the Beach.

'You may not want to eat those.' Marnie made a face. 'They've probably been around since we were in high school. You sure you don't want a drink?'

'I want to keep my head tonight.' There was no way I would chance a brain-damaged baby. A healthy one frightened me enough. The bar was packed with people I half recognized. It was Wednesday night. A handful of people nodded in my direction. A few came to the table and exchanged small talk— *Well, well, Zoe Lemonopolous, long time no see.*

Marnie and I had been there for nearly an hour when he walked in. 'Take a load off, stranger.' Marnie patted the chair beside her.

'Thanks.' Kyle leaned back in his chair confidently, talking to Marnie but staring at me. His easy lankiness and direct green-eyed gaze had always unnerved me. At the art show in Calgary I'd had the paintings to distract me from looking directly at him. Now that he was across from me, I had no choice but to meet his eyes.

It was a mistake to invite him, particularly since Calvin and I were at such odds. The night of our most recent fight—the worst of our marriage—Calvin had found my cigarettes in my bathroom drawer hidden behind a box of tampons.

'What're these?' He'd held them out accusingly.

'What are you doing in my drawer?'

'I was looking for floss. What does it matter?'

'It matters that you were rifling through my things—' My heart pounded.

'Cut the bullshit, Zoe.' His face, normally calm, was pinched with anger. 'How could you even consider smoking now? What are you thinking?' He continued, not waiting for my answer. 'Do you have any idea how damaging this is to a growing fetus? You may not be sure you want the baby, but for fuck's sake give it a fighting chance.'

I'd been disgraced and felt defensive. 'You didn't even ask me if I was still smoking.' I'd confided in my doctor, who said quitting gradually would lessen the effects of withdrawal, and would be safe for the baby as long as I quit by the fourteenth week. I didn't dare tell this to Calvin. He wouldn't understand the pressure I was under, seeing it only as a major weakness in my character.

'I know you well enough to know you do whatever suits you.'

'If I'm such an awful person, why did you marry me?'

'I'm wondering that myself. Christ, I can barely look at you right now.' He confiscated the cigarettes, tucking them in his pocket, and left for his clinic, not speaking to me when he came home too late for dinner. In bed we lay facing opposite walls. I was filled with an inexpressible sadness, so deep it was easier to bury than accept. His earlier words confirmed what I'd always suspected—that he considered me a huge disappointment.

He was right to be angry, of course. But rather than own up to my behaviour, I pushed it away since any reminder of my careless nature brought up things from the past that I preferred to ignore. I'd worked hard to stop hating myself, and here was Calvin pushing me back into the maze of self-loathing. My impulse, honed over years of denial, was to resist his criticism, which of course meant resisting, even resenting, *him*.

I was angry, too, with how quickly he'd rejected me. I was lonelier than I'd ever been, lonelier even than in my youth when the throbbing cycle of rejection and withdrawal had begun. Just as I'd done then, I withdrew—telling myself I didn't care. But the predictable lump in my throat told me otherwise.

Now Kyle and I are parked in Marnie's driveway after dropping her off. Her split-level bungalow reminds me of the Calgary subdivisions I always get lost in. Calvin and I rarely venture from downtown where we live. Along with everyone else we know who lives in the inner city, the value of our house has skyrocketed and we're willing to pay the ridiculous property taxes in order to hold on to our investment.

'What?' Kyle smiles, amused by my reaction to the plastic Jesus. 'What's so funny?'

'I haven't seen Christ hanging from a car mirror for years. Do you still have a crucifix above your bedroom door?' I squeeze Jesus in my hand to warm Him up. Kyle's headlights are turned off. 'Not anymore. It frightens the girls away.'

I let go of Jesus. 'You have a lot of girls, then?'

He takes a drag from his cigarette. 'Does that bother you?'

'I'm not exactly in a position to mind.'

'You can mind a little bit.'

'You never get entirely over those feelings, I guess.'

He stares at his fingers resting on the steering wheel. 'That's true.' His fingernails are clean white moons.

'Enough true confessions. Anyway, what does it matter now?' Most of the houses on Marnie's street are unlit except for a tan duplex still decorated with Christmas lights that spell out *Welcome Santa!* The winter snow has begun to melt away, revealing brown patches of dead grass. The air at this time of year is both fresh and foul. The smell of things decayed will only disappear with a complete change of season.

'It feels like we're back in high school,' I say. 'As though we're going to break our curfews soon.'

He chuckles. 'Christ. Imagine being eighteen again.'

But our lightness doesn't mask the fact that we're acting like self-absorbed adolescents.

'It's almost midnight.' He looks at his watch.

'You need to get home, I guess.'

'I have a babysitter. She can wait a while.' He turns the key in the ignition and looks at me. 'Want to go for a drive?'

I cup my hands between my thighs for warmth and look out the window, not wanting to appear eager. 'Where to?'

He backs out of the driveway. 'How about the Dumping Ground?'

'I haven't been down that way for years.'

'Well, it's still there.' He guides his truck down Concord's main commercial strip, past the new Tim Hortons, the Boston Pizza and the A & W where Marnie and I worked in the summer of 1984 as car-hop waitresses, carrying trays wet with spilt root beer to customers who tipped with dollar bills.

He shakes his head. 'I had no idea how much I missed you.'

I turn away, shy, and squeeze my hands more tightly between my thighs.

He turns off the strip onto a stretch of rough pavement that is referred to derogatively by the locals as *Chinese pavement*—a cheap version of paved road where oil is sprayed on gravel to keep the rocks down. The last time we were on this road together we were heading back to my parents' house from Bitter Lake, unaware of what was waiting ahead for us.

As though reading my conscience he clears his throat and says, 'I saw your sister the other day. She seems good.'

'Yes. She is.'

'I'm glad.' He looks ahead.

This is it, finally—the unspeakable event.

Kyle frowns. 'Cam called me up a few years ago. Wanted to borrow some money. I told him no.'

'You actually talked with him?' I ask, incredulous.

'I didn't *talk* with him. It was a short conversation, that's all.' He sighs. 'Listen, what happened with your sister was fucking awful. But forget about Cam. He's a drunken prick. You say your sister's doing okay, right?'

'Well, yes. But she's had a hard time getting there. A very hard time.'

'There's nothing we can do to fix things, you know that. Cam's not worth discussing.' He puts his hand on mine.

I pull my hand away. 'So that's it then? It doesn't bother you?' I hear the disappointment in my voice, thick and accusing.

He sighs again. 'What do you want me to say? That I feel bad? Jesus Christ, of course I feel bad.' A pause. 'But we can't change it, can we?' He glances over.

'No.'

'Are we going to spend our time talking about it? I will if you really want to.'

I gaze at the dark landscape. 'I'm not sure what that would even accomplish.'

He takes my hand again. 'Good.'

By not pulling away I offer my silent agreement, feeling as though I'm betraying my sister all over again.

Calvin is always saying, *You're so guarded with your sister. If you showed a bit of yourself to her it would make things easier. Be vulnerable for once.*

What he doesn't understand is that it's not that my sister doesn't know me—it's that she can't forgive me for what happened. As for being vulnerable, I've learned it's often safest to remain unattached—

Recently I turned the twelve-week-ultrasound photo of the baby down on the bureau where Calvin had propped it against a photo of us taken on our Mexican honeymoon.

'What's going on?' He frowned when he saw the photo.

'Nothing,' I replied. 'It must have fallen.' Every time I passed the bureau on my way to the bathroom I avoided looking at the baby, whose sunken haunting eyes followed me as though the photo were a trick painting.

The honeymoon photo made me sad with the way Calvin's hand rested confidently on my rib cage just below my breast. Today there is hesitation in the way we touch each other, or even talk. Most nights Calvin takes his plate of food to the living room to watch sports on television while I eat at the kitchen table, refusing his offer to help clean up. 'It's fine,' I call out to him. 'Just a few dishes, watch your game.' I stand at the kitchen sink rinsing dried-up food off the dishes and catch my image in the darkened window: *How on earth have I come to look so alone?*

Kyle pulls over and turns off the headlights. The red and yellow lights of the dashboard give the only light. The radio plays Duran Duran's 'Hungry Like the Wolf'. He turns up the music. 'Do you remember this song? Everything from the eighties is hip again. I guess that means we're officially old.' He leans back, his head against the headrest, singing along.

'You remember the lyrics. Not bad.'

He holds the cigarette pack toward me.

I shake my head. 'I've really got to quit.'

'How about some of those eighties expressions?'

I laugh. 'Don't have a cow, man!'

'Eat my shorts!'

'Gag me with a spoon!'

He leans back in his seat, his arm on the armrest touching mine. We stare out together at the nothingness. In my Calgary neighbourhood there is never a truly quiet moment. There are always sounds of cars driving by; people walking and talking; ambulances howling down residential streets. The noise of the city distracts me from my inner turmoil, which churns itself into a hyper-need for work and order. But here with Kyle, I feel a thrill that makes me feel alive, instead of merely busy.

'So.' He breaks the silence. 'What are we doing tonight?'

'What do you mean?'

'You know what I mean.'

'I just wish the world would stop for a moment. That I had only myself to consider without feeling guilty.'

He runs the steering wheel through his fingers. 'Everyone feels that way sometimes. Kara would rather pass out pretzels in business class than be here with me and Melanie. She says Concord is too small-town. Does she think I like it here?'

'I'm sorry,' I say, irritated with myself for apologizing. I pull on the door handle and step out of the car, squinting at the peaks of garbage in the Dumping Ground in the distance. In a hundred years the rubbish will all be buried deep below the surface. The same is true of our own petty troubles.

'Get in, okay? There's nothing to see out there.'

I get back in the car and fasten my seat belt.

He pulls onto the rough pavement. The car drops into a deep rut and it feels, for a second, as though we're pitching forward. Jesus twirls in an absurd pirouette.

'Where are we going?'

'We can always go back to my place.' He shrugs his shoulders as though it's a casual suggestion.

'We don't have to do anything. Just talk, right?'

'That's up to you.' The car's underbelly settles into the grooves of the road. Jesus spins to face me. His expression is contorted by cramps of agony. My mother would be appalled by my behaviour—would tell me to *wise up*; to treat my husband *with respect*. But right now I don't want to be wise. I don't want my loneliness, either—I just want the distraction of someone who doesn't expect anything more from me than the reciprocation of my feverish mouth.

I follow Kyle to the front door of his house telling myself nothing's happened yet.

'Bloody door handle.' Kyle pulls at it. 'Never works properly.'

'It's fine,' I say, as though I need to make him feel better. He gets the door open and we step inside. In Kyle's entryway there is a jumble of pink girls' sneakers and steel-toed boots sharing space with a pan of cat litter. I think of my own home in Calgary, my shoes arranged neatly inside the coat closet on a pine Ikea shoe stand.

'It's a mess,' he acknowledges.

I ignore the smell of cat litter like I ignore the flashing red signal in my brain. I'm fooling myself into thinking this won't mean anything, using my problems with Calvin to justify what's about to happen. Kyle moves toward me; our torsos collide in a mutually greedy embrace.

'What about the babysitter?' I whisper.

'Don't worry. She always falls asleep on the couch.'

'I don't know about this,' I mutter weakly, overcome by the gentle web of his fingers around my neck. But I *do* know this—for years Kyle and I have been denied each other. For now I will sweep the existence of everyone else from my mind, and allow myself to feel something besides my aching disquietude.

Six

When we move to Concord in the summer of 1981, one of the first things I notice is that the night sky appears brighter than the sky in our old back-yard in Edmonton. My father explains this is because there's less pollution in the air to block the light. 'Life's better for you in a small town.' He stares at the night sky through the large picture window, placing one beefy hand on Dorothea's neck and the other on mine in an unusual show of affection. He is pleased with himself for providing us with a home of our own, I can tell. I share his sense of anticipation. Perhaps things will come easier now, especially for my mother, who is difficult to please.

She pulled off her rubber gloves and tossed them on the countertop when my father announced we were moving to Concord to buy the Parthenon Pizza and Steak House. 'You see, girls,' she told us, gesturing at the nicked rental-house furniture and peeling linoleum floor, 'I told you things would improve.'

'Things haven't been so bad here,' my father argued.

'*Please.*' She rolled her eyes.

Since the move, my mother has busied herself hanging curtains and lining drawers with lavender-scented paper, humming contentedly while she works. She has taken up aerobics again, stretching in front of the tele-vision each morning in a burgundy Danskin leotard and turquoise leg warmers. 'Christ almighty,' my father says when he comes to the kitchen for his morning coffee. 'Put some goddamn clothes on.' She ignores our gig-gles and points breathlessly to the cereal boxes from which we are expected to serve ourselves.

One Friday night, shortly after we arrive in Concord, my father drives us all downtown. Dorothea and I are transfixed by the flashing lights of the Night Owl Arcade, where teenagers dressed in dark clothes hang around the entrance. In Feldman's Department Store my father tells my mother, 'Buy something. Anything you want.' We've already eaten egg rolls and chicken chow mein at the Golden Dragon, washing our food down giddily with grenadine-tinted Shirley Temples and splitting open the claws of our fortune cookies.

My mother sighs. 'We have so many things we need to buy, Costa. It's really not necessary.'

'Who said anything about necessary?' He thumps his chest with his hand. 'For once I wanna buy my wife a present and she refuses.'

'C'mon, Mom,' I say.

'Yeah, c'mon,' Dorothea pleads in the simpering tone that always sways our mother.

'Oh—' My mother touches the bevelled edge of the jewellery display counter. 'Well, maybe just a look.' Her lips crack briefly into a smile but she stops herself, as though she won't allow herself to be excited. She peers through the glass. 'What do you girls think?'

There are milky-blue opal pendants, birthstone rings, gold-plated ankle bracelets. Fat-linked silver chains are draped around the necks of headless mannequins. Freshwater pearls lie in coiled strands inside foil gift boxes.

We ignore it all, pointing to the large oval mood rings which are the latest craze.

'You ready?' The clerk pushes herself off her stool and plucks a ring from its foam tray. 'It's black right now because it's cold.' She slips the ring onto my mother's middle finger and plops back on her stool. 'Give 'er a minute to warm up.' We stare at the ring as it blossoms fern green. 'You have mixed emotions—that's common.'

'It's a gimmick.' My father folds his arms across his chest.

'The girls love it.' My mother holds out her hand as though admiring a diamond solitaire.

We nod vigorously, knowing better than to beg.

'We'll take it,' she tells the clerk.

My father slowly cracks open the leather compartments of his wallet. 'You're sure?'

'Positive.' She kneels down so Dorothea and I can rub the stone, letting us take our time. We are used to getting out of her way to play by ourselves while she sweeps crumbs, folds laundry and wipes fingerprints from cupboard knobs. *In a minute*, she always promises when we want her attention, but by the time she finishes her chores it's always too late.

'That ring's gonna stop working,' my father grumbles as we walk to the car. 'You'll see.'

'Oh Costa.' My mother slides into the front seat and yanks her seat belt across her lap. 'Don't spoil this now.'

I feel the tightening in my stomach that comes whenever my parents start to fight. I nibble the cuticle of my thumbnail nervously, ignoring the sting that comes when I tear away a strip of skin with my teeth. Dorothea stares at me anxiously as though she believes I can stop their bickering. I look away, fixing my gaze on the row of eyeglasses staring back through the window of Peeper's Optical. My thumb smarts with pain.

My father looks at us through the rear-view mirror. 'You girls like the ring?'

We nod mutely. I've already resigned myself to disappointment. I have been fooled by the aerobics, the new curtains and the brightly lined drawers. What was I thinking, believing things could be different here in Concord?

'All right.' He reaches back to pat our stockinged knees. 'We're not gonna worry about it.'

The car rumbles to life signalling that we are headed home. Unlike our rental house in Edmonton, with its basement tenant and Saran wrap stretched over the windows to keep out the drafts, our new home in Concord has what my father calls *every convenience*. Perhaps this will be a new start. A piece of fortune cookie dislodges from my tooth, providing me with a sweet, unexpected surprise. Air blows through the car vents, reaching our faces—cool at first, then comfortingly warm.

Seven

My modern new junior high school in Concord is six blocks from our house. My school in Edmonton was built of sandstone with separate entrances for the boys and girls—the kind of building whose hissing radiators spelled *old style, out-of-date*. In Concord there is a new leisure centre where Dorothea and I can take batik tie-dye classes or learn to curl. That's the beauty of living in a small town, my father tells us, where opportunities are close at hand.

According to my mother, the restaurant is the beginning of better things. But it means we'll have to *grin and bear* the hard work ahead of us—wiping spills from countertops, being nice to customers, going without new clothes until the restaurant is *up and running*. Dorothea and I are expected to help out by bringing menus and glasses of iced water to customers on weekends, and to keep quiet while our father sleeps late on Sunday mornings. We nod our heads in agreement, our eyes wide with wonder at the machine that dispenses Coca-Cola and Orange Crush from spigots with the simple push of a finger.

With its velvet drapes and dark wood panelling, the Parthenon Pizza and Steak House looks like every other Greek family restaurant. Thick-armed chairs squat at the edges of tables topped with scalloped paper placemats. Red plastic carnations sprout lopsidedly from cheap glass vases. The ornately patterned carpet runner is discoloured from the lunch traffic of businessmen in wet galoshes and high school students in dirty white Sorel boots who smoke and drink endless cups of coffee so they won't be asked to leave.

At home I sleep on a mattress without a box spring until we can afford a proper bed from the Simpsons-Sears catalogue. Even though my room is mostly unfurnished, I keep it neat by making my bed and keeping my clothes folded. Every morning before I get up from my mattress I trace the faded violet pansies of my bedroom's wallpaper with my fingertip and imagine how the mauve organza curtains my mother is sewing will look against the flowers. When I crawl onto my mattress in the evening my thoughts drift excitedly to the upcoming school year.

But the suspicious faces that bob up to look at me when I arrive late in

Mrs Crabtree's grade-eight classroom on the first day of school make me wish I were back in my bedroom, alone.

'Is this where you belong?' Mrs Crabtree asks impatiently. I nod wordlessly, unsure where to sit down. I am late from having to walk Dorothea to her elementary school. Everyone is already seated.

She points to the back row where there are empty seats. 'Hurry along, then.' She claps her hands sharply. 'We can't wait all day for you.'

The faces turn to watch as I make my way to the back. I look straight ahead so I won't attract attention from the long-haired boys with Nike high-top sneakers sticking into the aisle. The girls sitting together in the front row snicker at my patent-leather Mary Jane shoes. It's with new eyes that I understand the shoes are the type a grade schooler would wear. I'm also aware that my cardigan sweater is all wrong. The front-row girls wear grey flannel kangaroo jackets with hoods, their sleeves pushed casually to their elbows.

When lunch hour comes the front-row girls stand in a circle around my desk. The prettiest one introduces herself. 'I'm Kara. This is Marnie and Janice.'

'My name's Zoe.'

'That's a funny name.'

'It's Greek.'

Kara's mouth forms a small smile. 'You mean the country?'

'Uh-huh.'

'That's ... interesting.'

Was it good to be interesting? I grip my pencil case tightly.

'Did you go to a big school before this?' asks Marnie, whose eyebrows are darker than her straw-blond hair, giving her an uneven look. 'Were you popular?'

'I don't know ...'

'How can you not know if you were *popular*?' Janice cries in disbelief. 'Everyone knows if they're *popular*!'

Kara moves the gold star pendant that hangs around her neck back and forth on its chain. 'Are your parents rich?'

'I don't think so ...' I think about the way my father grumbles whenever my mother asks for money to buy groceries.

'Girls, it's time for lunch, let me have a few minutes of peace.' Mrs Crabtree makes a shooing motion with her hands.

'Let her come with us,' Marnie tells Kara. 'She's all right.'

Kara stares at my shoes. 'You'd better get your lunch if you want to eat with us,' she says finally, as though she's speaking to the shoes. 'We don't invite just anyone, you know?'

I rush to get my lunch from my locker. I can tell by the way the other kids look at me when I sit down that this is the popular group. In my old school in Edmonton, there were hundreds of kids. Here, it's easy to figure out that Kara is one of the leaders.

Kara sits at the head of the table, her lunch spread out neatly in front of her. Janice and Marnie sit on either side. Their three heads are bowed together over their sandwiches like praying mantises.

I pull my own sandwich from my bag. The girls look up and burst out laughing. I smile stupidly, unsure what the laughter is about.

Kara smirks at my sandwich. 'Nice wrap job.'

I look down, realizing they're laughing at the used plastic produce bag from the Co-op that my mother—too cheap to buy lunch Baggies—had used to wrap my peanut butter sandwich. Kara's sandwich is a perfect cellophane-wrapped square. I laugh with them as though to say, It is funny, isn't it? The peanut butter sticks to the roof of my mouth. I force the sandwich down, unsure whether it's the bitter lump of undissolved baking soda in my mother's homemade bread, or the anxiety in my throat, that makes it difficult to swallow.

Staying in the popular group takes all my attention. The girls notice things about each other I've never paid attention to before. They compare test scores to see who has the highest mark, acting like it's dumb luck if they do well. 'I guessed the answers,' says Janice, who's always the most anxious to fit in.

I'm careful to do well, but not so well that they call me a show-off.

'You can do better than this,' my mother says. 'You used to be a straight-A student.'

'It's tougher in eighth grade,' I reply. 'You have no idea.'

'Try harder,' my mother scolds. 'I don't have time to watch over your homework.'

When it comes to clothing the girls have no pity. 'What's that?' they shriek at the slightest offence—skirts that fall below my knee, elastic hair scrunchies that slip loose, baggy blue jeans from K-Mart bought by my mother, who doesn't understand the importance of designer labels. I'm not spending more money on your clothes than on my own, I can promise you that.

'What's wrong?' she asks when I refuse to wear my tan khakis. 'You picked those slacks yourself.'

'I don't *want* to wear pants,' I complain, not telling her that Kara's decided we'll all wear skirts today. I pray my mother won't insist I wear the pants. The girls will see it as a sign of rebellion and punish me with teasing.

'I don't know what's gotten into you these days.' My mother throws up her hands, too busy ironing her white polyester blouse for a shift at the Parthenon to argue. 'Wear what you like. Just make sure it's clean.'

It's nerve-racking to follow Kara's rules but I'm glad to be accepted into the popular circle instead of hanging at the edges of the crowd as I had in Edmonton. A popular girl has chosen *me*, which has never happened before—although Kara's actions are confusing. Sometimes she slips her arm in mine as though we're best friends, whispering secrets about the other girls: 'Janice is so flat she wears a padded bra.'

She talks about Marnie, too: 'You should see her house, dishes left in the sink all day. My mother says it's a pigsty.' I feel sorry for Marnie, whose mother married another man when Marnie was seven, leaving her behind with her father in Concord. Besides, Marnie is the only one who ever stands up for me.

Other times Kara links arms with Marnie or Janice, leaving me to trail behind wondering what they're saying about my own family. The girls treat our house as if it's a museum—filled with oddities from the Greek blue glass charms with painted eyes known as evil eyes, or *mati*, hanging above the doorways to my father's old-fashioned tooth powder. They open my mother's fridge, shaking the plastic container of stringy yellow *kasseri* cheese and smelling the rice-stuffed grape leaves—*You actually eat this stuff?*

The only saving grace is Kyle Lipinski—

With his dirty-blond hair and lazy smile, Kyle Lipinski looks as if he belongs on the cover of *Teen Beat* magazine. He wears chocolate-brown corduroys and sits behind me every morning in Social Studies class. Occasionally he gives me notes to pass to his best friend, Cam, who sits to my right. 'Pass this on,' Kyle whispers when the teacher's back is turned. His voice is a breeze through a car window on a stifling hot summer day—an unpredictable pleasure that licks the back of my neck.

Most days after Social Studies I walk with Kyle and Cam to the picnic tables where the kids sit for lunch when the weather is good.

'Stuck up snob,' Kyle says about Kara, who sits on top of the picnic table, her sneakers taking up space on the empty seat below.

'Don't say that,' I tell him, secretly pleased.

'Why do you like her? All she does is gossip and talk about clothes.'

Sometimes I go to Kyle's house after school. My mother tells me to play nice—as though I'm eight years old instead of in eighth grade. She doesn't have a clue about what goes on in the Garden City Trailer Court where Kyle lives with his mother and his stepfather, Ray. She would be horrified by the barking Doberman pinscher chained to a flat tire on the front lawn of their neighbour's trailer; by the washer-and-dryer set three trailers away waiting to be toted to the dump since September; and by the afternoon beer-drinking that goes on in the Lipinskis' trailer.

The bowed screen door that opens into the trailer has not held up well to hundreds of openings and closings. The rest of the trailer seems equally flimsy. Through the thin walls of the bathroom I hear every word they say, which makes me realize my peeing can be heard in the kitchen where Ray swigs his beer and Kyle's mother fries frozen hamburger patties in an electric skillet. Kyle has an older sister, Pam, and a younger stepsister, Angel, who belongs to Ray. 'Broken family.' My mother is smug when she talks about them.

But Kyle treats Angel as if she were a real sister, saving her the miniature Dairy Milk chocolate bars given to us by the school on special holidays. The most I'll do for Dorothea is knock sharply on the bathroom door before barging in. I can barely tolerate the sound of her breathing when we watch television together in the basement. The sound of Dorothea sniffling when she has a head cold is enough to send me to bed early.

The trailer court is different in many ways from the new subdivision where we live, where the main road winds, like a silver satin streamer, through tidy streets named after trees. Our family lives on Maple Crescent, in a split-level bungalow painted white with royal-blue trim: colours of the Greek national flag. Indeed, there's a small Greek flag hanging on the back porch, the sight of which makes my father happy for a few brief minutes each morning as he looks through the kitchen window, dunking *biskota* into his coffee before leaving for work.

My father has a wet bar stocked with rarely touched liquor bottles whose labels face neatly outward. Kyle's family has a Styrofoam cooler on their kitchen floor to hold ice for Ray's Pilsner.

Our household has no pets. *All that hair? No thank you,* says my mother.

Angel's pet cat sheds black hair on every surface of the Lipinskis' trailer. If I wear white socks to Kyle's trailer my soles become covered with a mat of thick dark hairs.

I make sure to watch through the window for my father's headlights when he picks me up at Kyle's on winter evenings when I can't ride my bicycle. I pull my boots on quickly and hurry to the car before he has a chance to call for me at the trailer door like he did the first night he picked me up, distressing me with the way he talked in his thick Greek accent about the federal government's National Energy Program. Ray responded to his conversation with sarcasm. 'What good does it do to vote? The west is ignored no matter what. Have a beer?'

'No, thank you very much,' my father replied in his broken English. 'Is not enough time tonight.'

Ray crossed his arms in front of his chest. 'You gotta get back to the restaurant, I suppose? Duty calls.'

'Yes.' He prodded me out the flimsy door. 'These people,' he said as we drove past curtainless windows and cars without licence plates. 'What do they do for a living?'

'I don't know,' I said, even though I noticed everything that related to Kyle. These were things I could not share with my father, who was impossible to talk to.

Eight

My sleep is fitful, interrupted by panic that claws at the edges of my dreams. I struggle against wakefulness in the same way one struggles against bad news, coming to consciousness with a violent start. I make out the pattern of Kyle's red-and-tan-plaid bedsheets, soft against my cheek. Calvin will be fast asleep in Calgary sleeping on his side of our bed. The apple-green light of Kyle's radio alarm clock shows it is 4:31 a.m. I've been asleep for nearly two hours. I look beside me where Kyle lies sleeping on his back, one arm flung casually above his head, oblivious to the shattering world. I do not need to look under the covers to see that I'm wearing nothing. Shame crushes my chest like a brick.

I slip out of bed. Kyle shifts from the change of weight and reaches out with his hand to the empty space I've left behind. A grumble escapes his lips and he keeps sleeping.

On the other side of town my parents are either sleeping soundly in their king-size orthopedic bed, unaware that I've not yet made it home; or they are sleeping restlessly, waking each other with spasmodic jerks at any sound that might signal my arrival. They will not telephone Calvin; they would never let him know what a royal screw-up his wife is. If there is to be a confrontation it will be with me standing in their foyer, holding on to the stair banister and trying to slip my boots off while my mother stands at the top of the stairs, gripping her robe tightly at the neck and hurling criticisms in a hush so as not to wake the entire house!

I pull Kyle's faded Genesis World Tour T-shirt over my head and walk down the hall to the bathroom, shutting the door behind me quietly and pushing in the lock. If my parents hear me come in I'll say I stayed up late talking with Marnie and lost track of time. They won't be pleased I've stayed out all night but it will be preferable to the truth.

I sit on the toilet and stare at my feet, which are alabaster white from the chill of the floor tile. My toenails, painted Passion Fruit Pink, had looked colourful in the esthetician's shop but appear tacky in this poor lighting. *Cheap*, my mother would say. I reach for the roll of toilet paper that sits on the back of the toilet alongside a sticky tube of Crest toothpaste and a child's colourful plastic cup. I unroll a handful of paper and strain to empty my bladder. *Get the hell out of here, you fool,* I tell myself. But I lean forward, gathering my hair in my hands and battling my remorse. I'm here in Concord to try to get along better with my family, not mess up my life even more—

'You're sure you know what you're doing?' Kyle had asked me earlier, after he'd paid the babysitter, and then eventually led me to his bedroom.

'Things are complicated.' I flopped on my back on his bed and stared at the ceiling stucco.

'I hear Calvin's a nice guy.'

'Very nice. The nicest.' I knew I sounded sarcastic.

'You haven't been getting along?'

'Not lately, no.' I turned over on my side to see that on Kyle's bedside table were several plastic-framed photographs. 'Is that your daughter?'

He nodded.

'What's it like? Being a father.'

'Mostly good. But sometimes—'

'Sometimes what?'

'Sometimes it would be nice to live alone, to do whatever I want without having to worry about looking after a kid.'

'Don't you do what you want anyway?' I teased.

He laughed but there was a shade of annoyance in his eyes.

I touched the photo with my finger. 'She's very pretty.'

'She takes after Kara.'

'What does Kara look like now?' I'd last seen Kara fifteen years after leaving Concord, when Calvin and I had been in Banff for an Easter weekend.

Do you know her? Calvin asked when he noticed me staring.

No, I replied, pulling him by his hand into the Clock Tower Village Mall.

Kyle leaned over and placed a finger under my chin. 'Shorter hair. Still pretty.' His breath smelled of cinnamon mints. 'You're better looking, if that's what you're asking.'

I let him push my blouse up. *Sometimes* not *making a decision is the same as making one,* I could hear my mother saying.

'God,' he groaned as he found the front closure of my bra. 'You always had such great breasts.' He kicked his jeans and socks off quickly as though he couldn't wait. In Kyle's bureau mirror our naked bodies still looked young and as though we belonged together.

In jeans my abdomen appeared flat. Naked, it showed a slight bump that looked out of proportion with the rest of my body. I put my hand instinctively on my belly.

'Am I hurting you?'

'It's not that.' I shifted away from him.

'What is it?' He looked puzzled until he noticed my hand. 'You're not pregnant?'

I stared at him, mortified by his discovery.

He pushed himself up on his arms. 'Shit.'

'I'm sorry, I should've told you.'

'It's not what I expected.' He rolled to the side.

'I don't want you to think I'm a horrible person. It doesn't seem real to me yet. The baby, I mean.'

'Apparently not.' He reached for his beer, holding the bottle to his mouth for a moment.

'Say something.'

'I'm not sure what to say.' He frowned and turned away from me, placing his bottle on the bedside table.

I pulled the covers above my breasts. 'You don't think I'm attractive like this.'

He made a short laugh. 'I think pregnant women are sexy, actually.'

Sexy.

It had been a long time since I'd felt desirable. The last time Calvin and I had sex he'd been overly careful. 'Is this okay?' he'd asked, perching himself cautiously above me, leaning on his elbows.

I'd answered, exasperated, 'You're not going to hurt the baby, if that's what you're worried about.'

'Christ.' Calvin had rolled away. 'Talk about killing the mood.'

Now Kyle was making me feel untouchable, too.

I reached for my blouse. 'I don't want to make you uncomfortable. I'll go.' In all my fantasies I'd imagined Kyle would accept me.

He stared at me for a moment as though deciding what to do next.

I struggled with the buttons of my blouse, flustered and angry. Who did he think he was to act piously, when we both knew he was used to taking what he wanted?

After a moment he ran his finger cautiously up my arm. 'I have to admit, it's a bit of a trip.'

'You're bad, you know that?' I shivered with his touch, letting my blouse drop to the floor.

'Isn't that why you're here?' He grinned and pulled me forward by the hip so we locked together, the bump of my abdomen bulging slightly against his warm stomach. 'I just don't want you to do something you'll regret.'

'It's a bit late for that, don't you think? Anyway, it's not your problem.'

'I guess I don't need to worry about knocking you up.' He smiled shamelessly.

I went quiet.

'Sorry,' he said.

'It's awful,' I replied. 'What we're doing.'

The bedside lamp blazed beside us. With Calvin I always turned the lights off, worried he would uncover my most intimate flaws. But with Kyle I wasn't afraid of being exposed.

After a time Kyle pulled me even closer, hesitant with his body as though asking permission. I allowed his hands to discover what we both already knew—that I was miles away from being flawless. For the first time in months, I didn't need to apologize for my shortcomings. Was this part of the attraction? I pushed the question from my mind, captivated by his roaming hands.

The light in the bathroom is dim. I squeeze toothpaste onto my finger, brushing my teeth this way, rinsing with water and spitting into the sink. There is a noise; I look down to see the bathroom doorknob turning back and forth. I unlock the door to find a young girl in a pink nightgown.

'Hi there. You must be Melanie. Do you want to use the bathroom?'

'Who are you?' The girl stares at me. I'm surprised to see that we're nearly the same height. Her blue-grey eyes, steadfast in their scrutiny, are Kara's. Until now Melanie had only been an idea in my head—not a real-life girl who stood in front of me in her nightclothes, making me feel my early-morning presence was an intrusion.

I step out of her way and tug Kyle's T-shirt down to cover my bare legs. 'A friend of your dad's.' Then, speaking to her as though she is a toddler, 'Do you need any help?'

She smirks and shuts the bathroom door without responding.

I tiptoe into the living room. The leather sofa is cold against my thighs. There's no sign of a woman's presence—no blankets or decorative throw pillows piled high on the sofa. The coffee table holds a package of cigarettes, a lighter, a messy collection of *National Geographic* magazines. In many ways, this is a bachelor's pad. I hug myself tightly and hook my bare toes around the edge of the table.

Kyle appears in the archway between the bedroom and living room rubbing his eyes. 'Did you wake her?'

'She's in the bathroom. I was quiet, I swear.' I pause, then say, 'I think she was surprised to see me.'

He shrugs. 'Don't worry about it. She knows I have friends.' He cinches the belt of his robe and sighs. 'I guess we're all up now.' He walks to the kitchen and opens the cupboard door. I follow, shivering in the thin T-shirt. He stares at a row of water glasses. 'My head is killing me.'

'Is she staying?' Melanie walks into the kitchen and hugs his waist, staring unblinkingly at me.

'No, she's going home.' He looks at me. 'Unless you want to stay for breakfast.'

'If I don't get home soon my parents will be scandalized.'

He nods and says dryly, 'Your mother will send out the police.' He pulls down a box of Froot Loops and a cereal bowl.

'I'll walk. It isn't far. If I could just borrow a sweater—'

'Let me take a look, there's probably something I don't wear anymore.' There is a sound of drawers opening and closing in his bedroom. He comes back into the kitchen. 'I left an old sweatshirt on the bed. Don't forget your watch is on the dresser.'

I nod. The watch had been a present from Calvin on our wedding day. He'd tied a small red ribbon around the edges of the box. *I wanted to get something to last.* He'd smiled, pleased with himself, even though he'd only just started his own dental practice and could hardly afford it.

Self-loathing flutters like a moth in my throat. 'I have to get going.' I push myself off the sofa to search for my clothes, finding my cold jeans crumpled in a pile on the floor. I dress in the light of the radio alarm clock which has played retro '80s music all night. The beat of Fleetwood Mac's 'Second Hand News' will play in my head all day long.

I look around the room for a sign of Kara—a photograph, a pair of left-behind earrings tossed on the bureau—but I find nothing. Then again, Kara had always been one to leave when it suited her—in a twisted way, that was part of her appeal.

Kyle's sweatshirt lies folded neatly on the bed. I pull it over my head quickly and retrieve my watch from the dresser. It's fancy for my tastes: small diamonds encrust the thick gold bezel.

'Well?' Kyle stands at the front door, leaning against the door frame. He smiles easily, as though there's no reason to feel guilty.

We stare at each other for a moment. With my messy hair and streaked makeup, I know I look a mess. He has sleep lines from his pillow on his cheek. I poke fun: 'We've both looked better.' Out of view in the kitchen Melanie slurps her cereal milk noisily.

'You always look good.' He winks.

I step over a pink sneaker, flustered. Kyle's cat appears out of nowhere and brushes against my calf, making me jump.

He reaches for the door handle. 'I'll get that for you.'

In spite of my shame, I linger.

'When are you leaving town?' he asks.

'In a few days.'

'I'd like to see you again.'

I nod as though I'm in a trance.

Stepping outside, I look around furtively. Anyone seeing me leave could guess the situation. The sky is starting to hint pink, reminding me of the old saying: *Red in the morning, sailor's warning.* Judging by the wind, the weather is worsening. If I walk at a quick pace I'll be home in fifteen minutes. I walk to the end of Kyle's street, then over the train tracks and past the *Concord Times* office until I reach my parents' subdivision. Before I know it I'm peering through the amber glass window of my parents' front door to see if anyone is waiting up. My mother has left the door unlocked.

I slip off my boots and creep upstairs to my bedroom to undress without turning my light on. I lie in bed with the coolness of morning coming off my hair. I doubt I'll be able to sleep but when I open my eyes the clock reads 9:13 a.m.

I lie awake for a long time looking at the closed bedroom door, too paralyzed to move. I'm still wearing Kyle's sweatshirt. What was I thinking to act so selfishly, and with Kyle of all people?

I hear my mother say, 'It's time she woke up.' There is a purposeful slamming of a cupboard door.

Repulsed by what's happened, I'm also flushed with emotion.

Images collide with each other—

In the first, Calvin's face appears aged with anger and bitterness. Kyle's face crowds out his image. Then my parents appear, grim and unforgiving. Dorothea shakes her head with triumphant accusation. Melanie stands in her nightdress, a look of pity on her face.

The baby, its features not yet defined into a face but more an *idea* of a baby, nudges all the other images aside.

My mouth waters and I push myself out of bed to yank open the closed door, barely making it in time to the bathroom to vomit into the toilet's clean white bowl. I stand with my hands on my knees, sumo wrestler-style, heaving from the effort.

Dear God, what on earth have I done?

Nine

'You can't toss out everything.' Dorothea grabs the shower curtain decorated with starfish that I've removed from its rod.

'You must be kidding me.' I take it back, holding it up so she can see the film of soap residue. 'That's definitely for the garbage.' I've finally gotten to packing up my parents' bathroom. This is the room that repels and fascinates me. There are dozens of lumpy bars of soap made from leftover soap shards by my father, who wastes nothing. There's an assortment of dusty cotton balls and denuded Q-tips in the vanity waiting to be tossed away. Sitting on the sink counter is a glass jar filled with tap water where my mother's dental appliance soaks.

'Dad's freaking out that you're throwing away his old razors.'

'Well, tell Dad to talk to me himself.'

'He's seventy years old for God's sake. He doesn't know how to communicate.'

I toss the curtain into a black Glad garbage bag. 'That's the problem with this family—no one ever wants to be straightforward.'

'This is perfectly good.' Dorothea holds up a half-empty box of Kleenex.

'Do you want to pack the bathroom? If I'm not doing a good job you're welcome to take over.' I bury my hand in a velvet sack of Velcro rollers to find a tangle of hair.

She leaves, slamming the door.

I reach into the bathroom drawer to find my mother's old Avon cosmetics kit in its original pink box. This is even better than the empty glass giraffe I found earlier that used to sit on a doily on the back of the toilet, filled with Sweet Honesty perfume. I'd dropped the giraffe one afternoon while playing around in the bathroom when I was a kid. *It just fell,* I lied.

My mother had mopped up the perfume with toilet paper—*Oh, Zoe, you're always so quick to avoid blame.* The words had stung me back then and I'd been vengeful, flushing strips of paper towel down the toilet to clog the bowl. It surprises me to remember how spitefully I'd acted. Until now I'd only remembered my mother's stinging words.

The Avon kit with its slender fingers of lipstick in colours such as

Ruby Slipper, Cherub and Bijou makes me suck in my breath. I can still remember my mother's strict warning to *stay out of the makeup!* Even though I am supposed to be getting rid of things, my hand hovers reverently above the box. 'Mom, I've got the Avon box—do you want me to pack it?' I yell.

'The what?'

'The Avon box.'

She comes to the bathroom door drying her hands on a pea-green tea towel. 'That's got to be twenty-five years old,' she says. 'I wouldn't give that to the Goodwill.'

And there it is—

The crushing realization of something long disappeared without my noticing. If I were to open the plastic lid, the cream rouges would be shrivelled into dusty crescents of dull pink. The faded lipsticks would be as hard as rabbit turds. I struggle to find the open mouth of the garbage bag and dump the Avon box in to join outdated bottles of mineral oil and Nivea face cream. I'm wiped out from the events of the past twenty-four hours—as desiccated as the dried-out tubes of eye shadow whose turning caps I can still feel, as if it were yesterday, at the tips of my disobedient fingers.

So much has dried up with time.

I can remember when my sister adored me—trusting me to paint her small mouth with pilfered lip gloss. I'd been affectionate, too. The young girls sitting cross-legged in the bathroom with the door locked behind them and their knees pressing against each other's are different people today. How many times had I pushed Dorothea away when she wanted to play, ignoring the disappointment in her small hopeful face?

Dorothea's crushed ear is a physical reminder of my guilt. But there were so many other incidents—

One time my mother scolded me for not eating dinner: 'Have you been eating junk again?' she complained. 'Your blue jeans are getting so tight—indecent, really.'

I toyed with my creamed corn. 'I'm not hungry.'

'At least finish your meat.'

I pushed the chicken into my mouth and chewed. 'You don't have to make such a big deal out of everything.'

My father slapped an open palm on the table. 'The last thing I need to worry about is this nonsense at home.' He pushed his plate away and stood up.

'Where's Daddy going?' Dorothea wailed.

'He has to get back to work.' My mother stroked Dorothea's hair in a way she never did with me. She glowered at me. 'You see what you've done?'

Dorothea slid off her chair and ran to her room to play with her Barbie Dreamhouse bought second-hand at a rummage sale. I was sick of the stupid Dreamhouse with its pink window planters and plastic flowers. I often mocked Dorothea—*Life's nothing like your stupid pretend world.*

My mother removed my father's plate and rinsed it at the sink, shaking her head as if I were a huge problem. 'You think it's easy looking after children, day in and day out?'

'I can look after myself.' I pushed my chair away from the table.

'Where do you think you're going?'

'To my bedroom.'

'I'm speaking to you.' My mother followed me down the hall.

I shut my bedroom door and braced my foot against the bottom edge. 'It's my room.'

'Open up or you'll be sorry!' She pushed against the door, heaving until I let go. She stumbled inside.

'What do you want?' I refused to lose my cool like my mother with her bulging red face.

'I want you to stop acting like a spoiled brat!'

I threw myself on my bed and stared at the ceiling as though she weren't in the room.

She grabbed a *Seventeen* magazine from the floor and shook it at me. 'I'm done with you!'

I laced my fingers together at the back of my neck. 'You don't scare me.'

'No?' She reached over and slapped my face so hard with the magazine that my face swivelled away and my teeth clattered together. When I turned back to look at her, my mother was breathing heavily. 'Now look what you made me do!'

She staggered into the hallway.

I sat up, burying my face between my knees. I would not give her the satisfaction of hearing me cry. After a while, I yanked my bedroom door open and went in search of Dorothea, who looked up from her Dreamhouse suspiciously. 'What do you want?'

'Nothing.' I sat beside her on the carpet.

'Don't you have something better to do?'

'Not really.' I ran my finger along the Dreamhouse gable.

'I don't want to play with you.'

'No?' I fingered the plastic flower box.

'I mean it, leave me alone.'

I snapped the flower box off with my fingers. 'Fine with me.'

'Get out of here!' sobbed Dorothea, clutching her Barbie to her chest. 'I hate you!'

'Welcome to the club,' I said nonchalantly as I walked out of the room. That would show my mother, who always made it perfectly clear that she preferred Dorothea.

If my mother was done with me, then I was done with my mother.

I haven't thought about that incident for years. And about what happened later, when Dorothea had just turned fifteen. Well, I can barely stand to think about it.

I frown at the garbage bag stuffed with outdated toiletries, disturbed by my tendency to reframe my memories so the bad parts are someone else's fault. My tendency to dismiss my poor behaviour as justified. For so many years I've stuck to my version of the past, or not thought about it at all. Yet little has changed with my attitude, it seems. Clearly Kyle is another example of this—my mind's habit of excusing my petulant actions. Of telling myself it's Calvin's fault that I've turned away. I return to my task of sorting through the bathroom, uneasy with my sudden insight. In spite of my recent unhappiness with Calvin there's no fathomable excuse for what I've done. The only excuse I can come up with is that I got carried away in the moment. At this point, I could walk away from Kyle, and no one would get hurt.

My mother calls from the kitchen: 'I hope you're not throwing away everything. Besides, you need to eat something.'

'You were out late last night,' my father says when I come to the table after packing up the last of the bathroom. The newspaper lies in messy sections in front of him. He picks up a spoon to crack his boiled egg, his hand shaking.

'What's that supposed to mean?' I take the spoon from his hands. 'Let me do that.'

'I can do it myself.'

'Don't be silly.' I crack the shell. 'I'm here to help, remember?'

He spoons the wobbling yolk into his mouth, chewing slowly as though he has no teeth. For the first time I notice age spots that speckle the backs of his hands. White chest hairs poke through the top of his sleep shirt. He points his spoon in my direction. 'You should call when you're going to be out late. We worry you might be in an accident.'

'I was out with Marnie.' I unfold the front section of the newspaper in a loud rustle. 'There was nothing for you to worry about,' I tell my dad. I don't dare look up when I say this. Even though I've taken a shower and pushed Kyle's sweatshirt to the bottom of my travel bag, I worry I won't be able to keep the secret from my face.

Dorothea sits at the far end of the table ripping her toast into pieces.

'Marnie, huh?' My father scrapes the last of the egg from the shell and grunts at the sound of her name.

Dorothea pushes her chair back from the table. 'I have to get going.'

My mother wipes the countertop with a J-Cloth. 'There should be enough gas in the car to get you around.'

'You don't need your car?' I ask.

'With your father retired? No.' She dumps Dorothea's crusts into the garbage. 'Where would we go this early in the day?'

'If you're so concerned about Mom and Dad you should visit more often.' Dorothea zips up her jacket.

I ignore her.

My mother jabs a dirty knife into the dishwasher rack. 'I told you I don't need the car. Do you girls have to fight every time you get together? It isn't worth getting help packing if I have to put up with this all week.'

'We're not fighting.'

Dorothea hoists her purse over her shoulder. 'I have to get to class.' The garage door opens and closes with a whine.

My mother waves a fork in the air. 'Your sister doesn't have a husband like you do. She needs our help. You should be more understanding.'

I scan the business section of the newspaper and cram a corner of freshly buttered toast into my mouth so I won't have to answer.

'She doesn't have much luck meeting men,' she continues. 'She isn't the most confident person in the world. And there's the matter of Ryan.'

'Zoe was out with that Marnie last night,' says my father.

My mother leans heavily against the lip of the counter. 'You don't want your husband to wonder what you're doing at night while he's at home waiting for you.'

My father coughs phlegm into his cotton handkerchief. 'Greek girls should act properly.'

'I'm not Greek. And trust me, Calvin doesn't sit around waiting for me.'

'Greek enough.'

'Calvin phoned last night. I told him you were out with a girlfriend,' says my mother.

'Well, that's where I was, wasn't I? I'll call him when I'm finished eating.' I push away my milk, nauseated by the smell.

'Are you coming down with something?' My mother raises her eyebrows. 'I have ginger ale in the refrigerator.'

'I'm fine.' I fill a glass halfway with water from the kitchen faucet and make myself drink. There are cans of food left on the countertop by Dorothea, who hasn't finished packing them away for the Lutheran Church food bank. By my professional estimation there will be three more days of packing during which we'll be busy wrapping dishes, throwing away stale-dated packages of dried beans and rotini pasta, and pouring the final inch of whiskey down the drain. In the basement there are sloppy stacks of old *Chatelaine* magazines my mother has kept for recipes never attempted—ambitious pages detailing the proper way to remove the membranes from grapefruit (use a curved, serrated knife), or extract the stone from the flesh of an avocado (whack the middle of its heart with a butcher's knife and twist). No matter how often I've told her to weed out her magazines the stacks have grown higher, and now it's my job to clear them out.

It's eleven-thirty. If I call now I'll catch Calvin while he still has patients in his waiting room and won't have much time to talk.

'How was your evening?' he asks when he comes to the phone. He's being as polite as a stranger, no doubt reluctant to quarrel over the phone.

'Fine.' I wrap the telephone cord around my wrist. A rush of paranoia overtakes me. How can he hear my voice and not know?

I feel compelled to make a partial confession—'I was out later than I should've been.'

'You needed to blow off some steam. Has it been that horrible?'

Relief washes over me. Of course he doesn't know.

'Not really.'

'Well, hang in there. You'll be home in a few days.' His voice is remote.

I wrap the cord tighter until there are purple marks on my skin. 'Thanks for taking care of things,' I say, even though there's little for him to do at home. My shelves are perpetually stocked with neat pyramids of toilet paper, colour-coordinated boxes of Kleenex, storage containers that conceal their messy contents from view. Perhaps this is my way of caring for Calvin, keeping his life ordered and easy as though to make up for my detachment.

Worries about the baby have pushed me even further away: How will I care for a baby when I've never even changed a diaper? Will I resent the baby for waking me in the night, or Calvin for sleeping through it? And what sort of baby will I get? A baby with Calvin's personality, or a colicky, difficult baby who shares the worst of my DNA?

Nowadays, a simple walk down the street of boutiques close to our home can cause friction. We walked past the Chic Baby Boutique recently and Calvin pointed to a cherrywood crib in the display window. 'What about that?'

'It's a bit soon, don't you think?'

'I guess.' He took a sip of his Starbucks coffee and kept walking, his voice heavy with disappointment.

I imagined we would eventually move my desk out of the small room we used as a study, painting over the olive walls with a pastel colour. My neat files tucked into the bookshelf would be replaced with baskets of picture books and plush toys. Our carefully decorated spaces would become crammed with the baby paraphernalia of high chairs and bouncy seats. But it wasn't the lack of physical space that troubled me as much as the space that continued to grow between us.

Now, on the phone, Calvin clears his throat. 'What's to take care of? A couple of plants, that's it.' He pauses. 'I have a root canal waiting.'

'Sure.' The clock reads 11:35 a.m. Most likely Kyle is hungover and only just thinking of getting to work on his latest woodworking order. Perhaps he is thinking about me, or perhaps not. I hang up and look out the window where my father's Greek flag wavers to life for an instant.

I throw a bag of oregano, brittle and useless, into the trash more forcefully than I intend, leaving the rest of the kitchen to tackle later. All this thinking distresses me—the baby, Calvin, the future, all dangling by an elusive thread of *feeling*.

I head downstairs to get a start on the Christmas boxes. At dinner last night my mother had said to my complaining father: 'We don't need Christmas decorations, Costa. There's no room at the Vista Grande for a tree. The girls can split our old decorations between them.'

Nestled in the first box are salt-dough decorations painted by my mother; they now crumble at my touch. There are flaking metallic balls and crocheted snowflakes hanging limply from loops of thread. I shove them to the bottom of a Glad bag so my mother won't notice.

The night the tree went up had always been a good time for our family—my mother good-humoured, my father proud of the full tree he'd picked out from the Boy Scouts' tree sale. Dorothea and I skipped around him with excitement—

I want to put the angel on top!

No, me!

I pick fluffy bits of cotton snow from the antique tin-horse ornaments Dorothea and I had once dismissed as out of fashion, preferring the blinking lights of our friends' Christmas trees. I wrap the horses in tissue and place them in a shoebox. I tell myself Dorothea won't want them. She and I grumbled about so many of our mother's efforts—her hand-strung strands of popcorn and fresh cranberries, the papier mâché crèche created from newsprint. We'd pleaded for bright silver tinsel, squeezing the blood from the cranberries with ungrateful fingers in the hope that she would relent.

Upstairs, the sound of the garage door opening signals Dorothea is home again. There are sounds of keys being tossed on the hall table. After a few minutes I hear her feet hitting the steps to the basement.

'What's in here?' She goes straight to the shoebox I've begun packing for myself.

'Nothing. Just junk.'

'You're not planning on taking these?' She fishes out a tin horse and holds it in her palm accusingly.

'I didn't think you'd want them.' My voice wavers.

'Well I do.' She glares at me.

'Take the goddamn horses if they mean that much to you.'

'Don't worry, I will.'

I tie the neck of my garbage bag into a knot, suddenly desperate to get away.

Marnie had called earlier—*Come by for coffee. I want to hear what happened with Kyle.*

I'd agreed, both shamed and excited by the prospect of hearing his name spoken out loud. *I'll be there after I've got the basement packed.*

Now I can't wait to leave, even though there are precious mementos still scattered about the rumpus room carpet.

My mother narrows her eyes when I get upstairs and put on my coat. 'How long will you be gone this time?'

'I'll be back in an hour.' I plop the garbage bag beside the box of photographs that no one knows what to do with. I pick up my eighth-grade photo, cringing at the sausage-roll curls in my hair that no one had told me to comb out. My father had scowled at the blusher on my cheeks.

A girl your age doesn't need makeup, he'd said.

I knew he really meant, *Girls who are easy wear makeup.*

My mother had been right about the wool dress: *You won't last through the morning in that getup, it's too hot.* By the time the photo was taken my hair hung in limp floppy rolls about my shiny face. The other girls, dressed in Reebok sneakers and concert T-shirts as though they couldn't care less about their photographs being taken, had raised their eyebrows at my patterned tights, no doubt seeing a girl who tried too hard to get it right. The girl in the photo with the naive smile doesn't even look like me anymore. Yet in spite of her overcurled hair and perspiring upper lip, she still appears to like herself.

I slide my key into the ignition. The car smells of the miniature pine-tree air freshener that dangles from the rear-view mirror, uprooted. My parents' house grows smaller in the mirror. Soon a new family will take over the house. They'll hang new curtains and re-wallpaper, as my mother did all those years ago. They'll ask, *What's this?*, noticing the crack in the concrete foundation that grows wider each year even though my father has tried many times to seal it.

My mother opened every closet door when we moved in, marvelling at *all this space!* She'd practically danced from room to room, mentally calculating where our few pieces of furniture would go. My father, already proud with ownership, had stooped to pull spears of nuisance grass that found their way through the crevices of the walkway. 'Don't get carried away, Sophie,' he warned my mother. 'You can't order new furniture until we have the money.'

'I need to be reminded?'

Now they're getting rid of things they've worked a lifetime to possess. No longer will there be a need for guest linens or serving platters. No more Christmas or Halloween decorations. They can take only what is most important—wedding photos, Ryan's artwork, treasured books. My mother has limited the number of Greek keepsakes my father can bring to the Vista Grande: 'For God's sake, Costa, those evil eyes have been staring at me long enough!'

I pull out of the cul-de-sac, uneasy with the sense that I'm running away from my problems again. In Calgary the idea of spending time with my family had seemed a good idea for several reasons—the baby was coming at the end of the summer, and after that I'd be expected to visit more often. Memories of childhood had been pulling at me. Besides, my parents are ailing. Who knows how much time we have left? But now that I'm here I don't know how to behave around them. Even my body responds awkwardly—my legs move clumsily, my hands inadvertently bat forks and pencils to the floor. I feel like a bumbling giant whose blundering ways harm those I love. Better to get out of everyone's hair for a while. This is what I tell myself as I drive away, relieved by the distraction of Marnie and her two small children.

Ten

'Say hi to Mommy's friend,' Marnie tells the two young boys who cling to her legs staring at me wordlessly.

I squat down to say hello. The oldest boy clutches a fuzzy black orca whale with a ripped fin. The younger one runs away to hide behind a brown leather chair, peeking out as though he expects us to be watching.

'They don't talk unless they need something.' Marnie places the boys on the sofa and turns the television on to a children's program. The boys stare at the flickering images on the screen. 'So tell me everything that happened with Kyle after you dropped me off. No holding back. I'm serious,' she commands, directing me toward stools placed around a kitchen island that overlooks the television room. Her dark eyebrows are raised in an arch.

This is both the blessing and curse of a childhood friend—there's no need to put your best face forward. In a small town you were the person you'd always been, and always would be. Perhaps the people who knew you first also know you best. Perhaps they can help bring you back to the person you were meant to be before life's circumstances took over—that confident, happy girl in the eighth-grade photo.

'We went for a drive.'

'And?'

'Then we went to his place.'

Marnie's eyebrows gather into a frown. 'I didn't think you'd actually go through with anything.' She sips her coffee; her glossy plum lipstick leaves a greasy mark on the mug. 'I hope you know what you're doing. A relationship with Kyle wouldn't last more than a few weeks. You'd be unhappier than you are now.'

'Who says we're going to have a relationship? And why does everyone think I'm so unhappy?' But the smear of Marnie's lipstick on her coffee mug reminds me of the argument Calvin and I had last month about a tube of ChapStick—

'That's full of phthalates,' he'd said, grabbing the ChapStick as I applied it to my lips.

'Full of *what*?'

'Phthalates. The chemical compounds used to make plastic containers.

They leach into everything and cause cancer. Pregnant women in particular should avoid plastics. Like the container for this lip balm you're so used to slathering on your lips.' He opened my cosmetic drawer. 'While we're at it, you should get rid of most of this stuff.' He fished out my compact blusher.

I slammed the drawer shut, suddenly enraged with his concern for the baby without noticing that *I* needed his compassion. 'I don't need you questioning everything I do.'

He looked up, surprised. 'Why are you so angry? There's a mountain of research to back up the phthalate controversy. I'm just trying to help.'

'I don't need help.'

'Because you do such a great job of looking after yourself?' He'd slapped the ChapStick on the counter. 'Here you go, then. Happy for once?'

Marnie adds Sweet'n Low to her coffee. 'If things are so great with Calvin, why are you sleeping with Kyle?'

'Don't say it that way—*sleeping together*. It sounds so ugly.' My stool swivels unexpectedly causing me to grab the granite-topped island.

I anchor the stool with my feet. 'I feel horrible about what happened. You have no idea.' Over the day I've swung between remorse and exhilaration.

'So what happens now?'

'I don't know …' How many times have I pulled up Kyle's e-mail messages, searching his words for hidden meanings? Was the way he signed his notes with his first initial a sign of intimacy, or laziness?

Marnie continues, 'Maybe you're both just finishing old business—replaying karmic energy, you know? Making up for the past. Although I don't know why you'd want to go back there.'

She is referring, of course, to our relationship. She has no idea of our greater regret. It seems that how we handle what happens in adolescence is also how we handle what happens in our families—we carry the affliction forward, telling no one and pretending it never happened in the hope that it will fade.

'Have you been reading New Age books?'

Marnie lets out a short laugh. 'Just watching a lot of *Oprah* these days. What else is there to do for excitement?' She pours orange Goldfish crackers into two plastic bowls and fishes one out for herself before taking the bowls over to the children. 'You kids want juice?' They shake their heads, their mouths already dusty with orange powder.

'It doesn't take *Oprah* to figure out I'm messing with karma. Besides, you don't know the half of it.'

'What's that supposed to mean?' Marnie comes back to the kitchen island.

I shake my head. 'You'll think I'm awful.'

'You have to tell me now,' she practically wails.

'Fine. But you can't tell anyone. I mean it.' I find myself spilling out the news about the baby. Marnie's face closes up. The children come to pull at her but she waves them away, distracted. 'In a minute, kids, watch something else.' She picks up her coffee mug, takes a drink and sets it down with a sharp *clack* so it splashes coffee onto the granite.

She takes a moralizing tone—'You've created quite a situation, haven't you?' She stands up to get a paper towel. 'I'm sorry to be judgmental. I guess I don't know what you're looking for. You're not pleased about the baby?'

'It wasn't my intention to get pregnant.' Her reaction jolts me. Perhaps Marnie, with her messed-up childhood, can't imagine risking a peaceful home life for someone like Kyle.

'You and Calvin talked about whether or not you wanted children?'

'I guess. But we hadn't come to a decision.'

'How far along are you?' She looks at my stomach. 'You're not even showing.'

'Nearly four months.'

'Well, I guess you're keeping it.'

'Obviously.' I had assumed that over time I would get used to the idea—even excited. I'd been hoping I simply had cold feet. What was wrong with me that I didn't feel anything yet for the baby?

'You can't possibly think Kyle would raise the baby?'

I sigh. 'It's probably difficult for you to understand, but the baby doesn't really factor in any of this. It wasn't my plan to get involved with Kyle. I just wanted to see him again. I can't really explain it.'

She raises an eyebrow. 'You think you're soulmates, is that it?'

'Don't be silly.'

'But you do think that, don't you?'

'I don't know what I think anymore.' But I *had* been thinking that there must be something special between us to hold our attraction to each other all these years. It was as if I'd come home in two senses, not only to Concord but to Kyle. Coming back to him was revisiting the unguarded part of myself that existed when I was younger, before the awful affair with Dorothea.

How can I explain this to Marnie, who will tell me I'm acting like a teenage girl?

She stares at me before answering. 'Well, if you want my opinion, you're best to stop what you're doing right away. You always had a habit of focusing on Kyle to the exclusion of everything else.'

'You're right. Of course you're right.' I tell her what she wants to hear, fishing in my purse for my car keys. The night before I left Calgary I'd drawn a warm bath, sitting on the edge of the bathtub to test the water with my toe. According to my pregnancy book the water was supposed to be tepid so as not to overheat the fetus, which lay rolled like a fist in my womb. I'd run my other foot through the fluffy white bath mat, aware of the pleasant sensation against my toes. The rest of me was frozen with fear.

I lowered myself into the tub. My belly, with its subtle roundness, disappeared into the water. Soon the waistbands of my pants would seem to shrink. My body would become sturdier, able to support nearly thirty extra pounds. My bladder would become a nuisance, as would the onslaught of emotions.

I soaked for a long time before popping the drain open with my toe. The water funnelled noisily down the drain. I'd believed the events of my past were mostly over with. From an early age I'd learned to protect myself—but now this: a baby, who would require me to be vulnerable when I'd worked so hard to avoid opening myself up. The worst thing you could do to a child, I knew, was withhold affection.

She touches my hand. 'Please don't go. I don't want you to be angry with me.'

'It's not you I'm angry at.' I take a step toward the door. My family is waiting. 'I promise.'

If I am angry at anything it's not at Marnie, but at the idea that my carefully girded life is failing at the seams.

Eleven

At Concord Junior High I learn to be guarded.

One day, when I sit down at the cafeteria table, the girls pick up their lunch bags and move to another table, leaving me to force down mouthfuls of homemade wheat-germ cookies and struggle to keep my eyes from watering while everyone in the cafeteria watches. The girls sit at their new table creating an obnoxious amount of chatter as though to say, *Who needs that dumb Zoe Lemonopolous around anyway?*

I suspect it's a result of what happened the day before, when Marnie brought her Ouija board to Kara's house after school. While most mothers spend their afternoons folding laundry in front of the television, Kara's mother works with her father at the GM dealership they own. We girls spend afternoons unsupervised at Kara's house, mostly in her parents' bedroom. The Gunnersons' waterbed stands between chrome-legged bedside tables stuffed with Mr Gunnerson's dirty magazines. The bed farts when we roll about on its surface causing us to break into hysterical laughter. The emerald-green satin bedspread is cool against my cheek and smells of unwashed hair.

Inevitably our attention turns to the *Playboy* and *Hustler* magazines that show naked women with triangles of tawny pubic hair. The pictures create a warm, strange pulse in my lower body. I can't imagine my own father reading these magazines—although Kara's father does things I wish my father would do, like playing softball on the men's league and wearing handsome suits. Mr Gunnerson talks to me as though he's interested in what I have to say—asking me how school is going, am I pleased with my classes, do I like living in Concord.

I knew the Ouija board was black magic—in the same category as tarot cards and séances. My mother, who regularly dragged me and Dorothea to the Lutheran church, would have a fit if she knew I was messing around with the Ouija.

'Don't open your eyes, dopes.' Marnie showed us how to place our fingers lightly on the heart-shaped pointer. 'It won't work if you look.'

'You're moving the pointer on purpose with your fingers,' Kara accused her.

'Am not!' Marnie was the most likely of us to talk back to Kara, unlike Janice, who burst into tears at the smallest insult. Mostly, Kara and Marnie left Janice alone—*Don't bug her, she'll just run home and tattle.*

My mother had sympathy for Marnie: 'God knows no one else will look out for that girl. The nerve of her mother, leaving such a young girl alone with her father. No wonder he's always in the Parthenon's lounge.' I'd been to Marnie's rundown house behind the bowling alley, stepping reluctantly on the dirty carpet. 'You can keep your shoes on,' Marnie said, offering the only acknowledgement that the house was unclean. There was a sour smell from the unwashed plates that filled the kitchen sink and a pile of laundry sat, unfolded, on the sofa. But I didn't mind the mess because I preferred spending time with Marnie away from the other girls.

I opened my eyelids a crack, grateful for the squabbling between Marnie and Kara because it spared me. The room was dark except for a purple cat-shaped candle. Decorative candles had become very popular. Kara's mother, who was always the first to try new trends, had her hair done every month at the salon in a short pixie style while my mother wore her hair in a severe twist that showed the grey strands at her temples, which she never managed to entirely cover with drugstore dye.

'I'm not playing anymore if you make things up.' Kara leaned back on her hands and sulked.

Marnie rolled her eyes. 'Don't take everything so seriously.'

'Well, quit cheating,' Kara grumbled.

When Mr Gunnerson opened the door and flicked on the light to tell us it was time to go home we screamed and clung to each other in a fit of giggles, sending the pointer flying off the Ouija board to land at my feet.

Mr Gunnerson bent to pick it up, squeezing my calf and smiling at me. 'Here you go.'

'Get out of here, Dad!' Kara yelled. 'You're always butting in!'

When we left Kara's bedroom, Mr Gunnerson trapped me in the narrow hallway. 'You'll come back soon?' he asked, standing so close that I could smell the liquor on his breath.

I nodded.

He touched my elbow. 'Good girl.' His hand slid up my arm to press against my collarbone, where it was resting when Kara found us—

'What are you two doing?' Kara had snuck up on us. She stared angrily at me as the other girls came back into the hallway, curious to see what was going on.

I stepped back. 'Nothing.' The lump that was always in my throat when I played with the girls swelled so large I could barely breathe.

Mr Gunnerson dropped his hand and laughed sarcastically at Kara. 'You're just like your mother. Always seeing things that aren't there.'

'You're in big shit,' Marnie said, wide-eyed, as we pulled on our jackets and filed outside. She touched my mitten. 'You should be more careful.' The cool winter air went through my jacket, causing me to shake more than I already was.

After two days of eating lunch alone in the cafeteria, I escape to the library where I can sit unnoticed. I read the same paragraph in Judy Blume's *Forever* over and over again, even though I've been waiting for weeks to get my hands on the novel.

By the end of the week I'm summoned to the empty Modern Science classroom after school by Marnie, who finds me at my locker: 'Kara wants to see you.'

I enter Modern Science, forcing my lips into a false smile, humiliated to realize I'll forgive the girls if only they'll take me back.

'You don't understand what your *problem* is?' Kara leans against the teacher's desk shaking her head in amazement. She looks at the other girls. 'She really doesn't think she's done anything wrong.'

'But I *haven't* done anything wrong. Not on purpose.'

'The problem with you,' Kara says, 'is that you think you can do whatever you like because you're better than us.'

'That's not true!' My nails dig into my palms. They don't know I spend my evenings staring into the bathroom mirror trying on different expressions so I'll appear unbothered. Or that I spend every penny I earn at the restaurant to buy the same kind of clothes as my friends. Regularly I lie to my father about where to drop me off when I meet them so he won't embarrass me with the way he hunches over the steering wheel, peering at us suspiciously.

'You think because your parents own a restaurant you're more important,' accuses Janice.

Tears trickle down my cheeks. 'I don't think I'm more important. Besides, my parents don't own the restaurant. They make payments.'

Kara rolls her eyes. 'Quit creating such a big deal of things. You don't need to cry, we're all friends.'

The Modern Science classroom is full of stuff that I don't understand—rows of dark brown bottles that hold chemicals whose symbols I can never keep straight. My nostrils shrink from the stink of formaldehyde. The boys can always be counted on to handle the dissections. That's what I like about boys—they prefer to mess with animal innards instead of ripping *each other's* guts out.

'Pay attention,' Kara says sharply, rapping her knuckles on the desk.

'What do you want me to say?' I hear myself whining. The doors to the Modern Science room are shut tight to the outside world. If we're discovered by a teacher, Kara and the girls will smile sweetly as they always do—*We're just talking about our homework. Right, Zoe?* And I will nod in agreement.

'It isn't what we want you to say.' Kara stands with her legs apart. 'It's whether you want to improve yourself. I told you, quit crying!'

'I'm not crying.' I wipe my cheeks with the back of my hand.

Marnie looks surprised by my tears. 'Ease up,' she tells Kara.

Kara shakes her head as though our weakness disappoints her. She scowls at me. 'Can't you understand that we're trying to help you?' She signals to the other girls that it's time to leave. Soon the janitor will be pushing his wide broom down the hall.

I watch them walk away from me and realize that I'm holding my breath. When Dorothea and I were younger, our father taught us to swim the full length of the pool without coming up for air. We'd practised holding our breath until our lungs hurt. *The trick is not panicking,* he told us. *Believe you'll get to the other side, and you will.*

It seems like I've been under water for days, struggling to hold in my fear.

My mother blames me for the fact that the girls have quit phoning. 'You should be nicer to those girls,' she says when I come home early. 'They would invite you to their homes again.'

I know better than to tell my mother that the girls are still giving me the silent treatment despite our talk in the Modern Science classroom. If I tell my mother, she'll phone the principal and insist the girls get a talking-to. Or else she'll scold me without bothering to hear my side of the story. 'You're too sensitive,' she'll say. 'You've got to learn to get along.'

I unzip my snow boots. 'You don't have to worry so much about me—I'm not a baby.'

'You're not acting very grown-up, running around without a toque.'

My mother unloads groceries from paper bags, putting away milk and an enormous block of Velveeta cheese. She places a plastic container of alfalfa sprouts on the counter; she has read in *Reader's Digest* that the sprouts are full of vitamins. The snarled bunch of shoots will be ridiculed by my father — *We live in a goddamn hippie commune now? The next thing you know, we'll be eating vegetarian moussaka!* She folds a paper bag along its seam and places it in a drawer to reuse. She often tucks slightly used Kleenexes back in the tissue box thinking Dorothea and I won't notice. She points to my boots. 'Put those on the mat so they don't ruin the floor.'

'Why do you care so much about the floor?' I try hard to stop my voice from breaking. For days I've walked the school hallways alone. I feel myself giving in to the pressure, cracking like the shell of a soft-boiled egg. If I break open I'll be a messy leak of tears and mucous. The worst part is that I don't feel superior to the other girls as Janice has accused, but, rather, inferior in every way.

My mother shoves the drawer shut. 'Why don't you tell me what's really bothering you? Did your friends hurt your feelings? Don't forget those girls don't know everything.'

'They haven't done anything wrong. I can handle myself.'

'I hate to see you like this.' She reaches over to put a hand on my shoulder.

'I'm fine.' I push her hand away and hurry downstairs. Who does she think she is, trying to be nice? If I hate anyone it isn't just the girls, but also my mother, who made me wear a white thrift-store swimsuit to the Kiwanis pool for swim lessons in summertime, so transparent from use that it showed the cleft between my legs. Whenever I protested about the swimsuit my mother rolled her eyes — *Is there anything you don't complain about?*

For once I'm glad to see Dorothea in the rumpus room because it means my mother won't follow me downstairs to talk.

As usual, my sister ignores me, slumped into the sofa reading a book, with a blanket wrapped around her shoulders.

The rumpus room is a dumping place for our old junk: the dog-eared books on the lower shelves share space with odd knick-knacks — *Roots* by Alex Haley sits alongside a troll doll with stiff purple hair. Erma Bombeck's *If Life Is a Bowl of Cherries, What Am I Doing in the Pits?*, Dr. Atkins' *Diet Revolution* and *I'm OK — You're OK* crowd out our dad's collection of miniature nude Greek statuettes, which we've examined for clues to our own bodies. The Better Homes and Gardens *Fondue and Tabletop*

Cooking, which led to our mother's purchase of a mustard-yellow enamel fondue pot, sits dusty and forgotten beside a neon-purple lava lamp that drips giant tears of oil.

The clutter of the room irritates me but I can't go back upstairs. Annoyed with the crammed bookshelves, I push against the spines of the books so they're flush with each other. I plunk myself onto the sofa, as far away from Dorothea as possible.

'What's wrong with you?' asks Dorothea finally, looking up from her book. 'Your stupid friends got sick of you?' Dorothea doesn't have a clue about friends—her classmates are harmless little girls who still play with Barbies.

'What do you know?' This is the best retort I can come up with. In the room where my mother has begun tearing off the old wallpaper so it hangs in shreds, Dorothea and I sit wrapped in blankets that smell of mothballs and stale breath while I chew my bottom lip until it bleeds.

Twelve

By spring most of my spare time is spent with Kyle.

When I get home from spending afternoons at the trailer court, my mother is full of questions.

'What does the stepfather do all day at home?' she asks. 'Does the mother have a job?'

Kyle's mother works as a waitress in the Woolworth's cafeteria until four o'clock every afternoon dishing out daily specials and dealing with what she calls *pain-in-the-ass customers*. Her uniform is a pale blue dress made of polyester that *doesn't breathe, goddamnit!* and a pair of flesh-tone sandals that match her nylon stockings. When the weather is cold she wears a cardigan over her slumping shoulders. She hates the sweaty kitchen and the Polish cook who doesn't understand her when she passes along customers' requests for salad dressing on the side, or unbuttered toast. It is Mrs Lipinski who has to deal with the unhappy customers when the cook gets it wrong. *That's the final insult*, she's fond of saying.

Mrs Lipinski doesn't have *a lick of energy* to deal with her children after work, and so it's easy for Kyle to sneak cigarettes and beer, and for Pam to drive around town in her Indian boyfriend's Trans Am. But Mrs Lipinski often has time to ask questions about my family. 'Does your family speak Greece at home?' she asks as she rummages through the refrigerator for plastic-wrapped minute steaks. 'Or is it Greek? I always get mixed up.'

I answer these questions politely while Mrs Lipinski moves about the kitchen, occasionally sitting down to rub the arches of her feet with her thumbs. She says, 'If you find a man who'll rub your feet, marry him—trust me, it's the little kindnesses that add up.' Mrs Lipinski sneaks cigarettes from Ray's package, drawing them out carefully so her long fingernails don't break them in half. 'Don't tell Kyle, hon. I don't want him picking up my habits. It's bad enough his real father is a sorry piece of work.'

I agree even though Kyle has made me promise the same thing—*If my mother knows I smoke she'll tell Ray. All I need is for him to find another reason to be on my back.*

One afternoon, Kyle and I sit on a concrete speed bump in the school parking lot after the teachers have gone home. He uses a twig to draw pictures in the dust.

'There's nothing to do in this shithole,' he says. 'You wanna go to my place?'

For once I don't have to work at the restaurant. I've grown to hate work, having to wear a black polyester skirt with a high waistband that cuts into my skin. My white blouse quickly becomes soiled from reaching across tables to wipe greasy fingerprints from the plastic menus and refill bowls with small triangles of coffee cream.

Occasionally my so-called friends come in for coffee, but mostly they go to the Golden Dragon, where they can order free refills without being watched over by my father: *You girls gonna order something to eat this time?* While I am filling ice trays and brewing steaming pots of coffee that scald my arms, my friends are down the street giggling at the menu: *You want fried lice with your steamed eyeballs?*

I kick at loose rocks with my shoe and answer Kyle. 'I guess.' I push myself off the speed bump and brush the seat of my shorts with my hands. It's hot for May. The metal handlebars of my ten-speed scorch my fingers as we cycle toward the trailer court.

Kyle slows down at the entrance to Garden City. Ray's truck is parked in the driveway of their lot. 'It looks like Ray's home from the rigs again. Layoffs.'

'Is he going to be mad I'm here?' Ray has always been nice, calling me *half-pint* and telling me to fetch myself a cream soda from the Pop Shoppe box that sits beside the fridge.

'Nah, that's not it.' He grips his handlebars tighter. 'He's going to be pissed when my mom tells him Pam's been dating an Indian from the reservation.'

I'm uncomfortable around Kyle's older sister, who wears too much eyeliner and jeans that are so tight they leave little to the imagination, as my mother would say. 'Maybe we should go back to the school.'

He gets off his bike. 'If they start fighting, we'll take off.' He pulls at the screen door.

'Hi, half-pint.' Ray's voice is slurred. There are four empty beer bottles and an ashtray overflowing with Craven 'A' butts on the Arborite table in front of him.

I hug the door jamb with my body.

He pats the chair beside him. 'Don't hide over there.' Mrs Lipinski and Pam sit across the table. Pam's hair is the same dirty blond as Kyle's, but streaked lighter by days spent tanning on the patch of grass that is the trailer court's park. Pam spends entire afternoons lying on her towel alongside her best friend, Natalie, who with her dark, exotic looks is the opposite of Pam, although equally beautiful. Rumour has it that Natalie is part Pakistani—what some of the kids call *Paki*. The girls undo the strings of their bikinis when they tan, prompting the trailer court boys to dump buckets of cold water on their naked backs in the hopes of getting a glimpse of breasts. 'Jerk-offs!' The girls jump up, hugging their bikini tops to their chests. 'Get a life, assholes!'

Ray asks, 'You're not afraid of me, are you?'

'No,' I lie, letting go of the door jamb.

'Sit down, half-pint.' He slides the empty chair closer to him, burning his finger as he retrieves his cigarette from the ashtray. 'Damn.' He waves his hand to shake away the pain. 'So tell me—what do you see in my stepson?' He leans toward me as if we're sharing a private joke. 'He thinks he's some kind of artist with his fancy drawings.'

I look at Kyle, who's getting a Canada Dry from the refrigerator and pretending not to listen. I know Kyle tries to keep his sketchbook hidden from Ray, who makes fun of his drawings. When Ray isn't around, Kyle always seems to be sketching.

Mrs Lipinski jumps to her feet with a lightness I hadn't realized she was capable of, and says in an overly bright voice, 'Who'd like a Mars bar? There was a special at the department store.'

'Thank you.' I never get chocolate at home. I pull the plastic wrapper off the candy, sinking my teeth through layers of waxy chocolate, caramel and fluffy malted milk. For a moment I forget my unease with Ray as I press a melting chocolate fragment to the roof of my mouth with my tongue.

Kyle sits in his mother's empty seat. 'Zoe and I are just friends.'

Ray raises his eyebrows sarcastically. 'Just like your sister is friends with that Indian who drives the yellow Trans Am. It's bad enough we gotta see those Nitchies in town, now they're driving nicer cars than the white people.'

'It's the native oil rights.' Mrs Lipinski sweeps crumbs from the table with her hand. 'Why shouldn't the Indians be compensated for their land?'

'You want your daughter dating a Nitchie? You know they all want white women. It's a prestige thing.' He points his cigarette in my direction. 'What do you think about this nonsense?'

Kyle speaks up. 'Leave her alone, Ray.'

'Zoe can talk for herself.' He waves his cigarette at me. 'Isn't that right, half-pint?'

'Yes,' I answer feebly. What's left of the chocolate bar slips from my nervous fingers.

Mrs Lipinski busies herself clearing coffee cups and beer cans from the table.

I wipe the chocolate from the floor with my serviette, picking up cat hairs.

He continues: 'How's your father doing with the restaurant these days? Business isn't so good, is it? It's not just the laid-off rig pigs like me who can't afford anything these days. Fuckin' Trudeau and his National Energy Program, French fucking bastard.' He cracks open another can of Pilsner and leans back in his chair revealing an unzipped fly. He points a finger at Mrs Lipinski: 'Don't you start nagging me about the beer.'

'I should get home,' I tell Kyle, folding the serviette and putting it in my pocket, too frightened to walk across the kitchen to the trash can.

Mrs Lipinski puts her arm around my shoulder and walks me to the door. 'We'll see you later, honey.' I make my way down the rickety steps. I'm brushing aside the quack grass at the side of the trailer to unlock my bicycle when I hear Ray's angry voice through the screen door.

'You quit bringing that girl around. Her parents will start complaining.'

'She doesn't come over much.' Kyle's voice is meek.

'It's bad enough I have to raise someone else's kids, let alone feed your girlfriend.'

Through the sheer drapes I see Ray leaning across the table toward Kyle so their foreheads almost touch.

'She's not my girlfriend.'

'She's not my girlfriend,' mimics Ray. He stands up and chugs his beer, taking a step toward Kyle with his free hand raised. 'You won't talk back to me, you little shit, understand?' I quickly move away from the window, my fingers shaking so much I can barely make out my lock combination. If Kyle catches me listening he'll be ashamed. I yank my lock open. There's a *crash* from inside the trailer, then silence.

I make it to the end of the trailer court with my bicycle and then I stop to still my legs. When I look back Kyle is slamming the screen door shut and running in my direction. 'Shove over,' he commands. I slide to the back of my seat to let him pedal, realizing by the shaking of his back that he's crying. He pedals furiously until we reach the Chinese pavement where he stops, panting from his effort. He gets off the bicycle and walks to the edge of the ditch. I tilt unsteadily on the bike seat. He lights a cigarette and stares at the flat line of the horizon. 'Four more years to get out of this fucking town.' He throws a rock into the ditch. 'When I'm gone you won't see me for the dust I leave behind.'

I get off my bike and go to him, putting my hand on his back.

He slumps against my hand.

'It's going to be all right,' I say, with more faith than I feel.

He twists around and kisses me hard on the lips, his mouth salty with tears, making a whimpering sound before pulling away.

We stare at each other shyly, the toes of our sneakers gripping the edge of the ditch. For a moment, the fight with Ray is forgotten.

From that day on I can barely keep Kyle from my thoughts. Helping my mother dry dinner dishes or working in the restaurant filling sugar containers are tasks that merely interrupt my love for Kyle. And it is love. I have all the symptoms—the inability to concentrate, the hot cheeks, the nervous flu-like stomach. The time I used to spend mooning over my idols in *Teen Beat* magazine seems childish now. Without giving it a second thought I understand that I've grown up enough to land in the middle of a world where hands wrapped around a girl's waist are now allowed to come briefly under her sweater.

The thing I like most, though, is holding Kyle's hand. He doesn't often show his affection, but sometimes his fingers brush purposely against mine to gather them in a ball. It's tricky knowing what's in his mind. I catch him staring at me from across the cafeteria where he sits with the other boys. Other times he doesn't acknowledge me when I'm sitting right beside him on the gym bleachers.

When I ride my bicycle home from school I choose the paved path so I can ride no-hands, with my fists rammed into the pockets of my hooded fleece jacket. I'm happy at moments like this, when the smell of sun-dried grass pleases my nose, and I'm not trying to defend myself against my girlfriends, or avoid my parents, who seem more harried every day with the dwindling number of restaurant customers. I close my eyes and risk falling so I can shut out the passing landscape, which reminds me I'm pedalling away from Kyle—the only one who makes me feel as if I'm not alone.

Thirteen

I hardly ever talk about the girls of my adolescence to Calvin. Much like everything else that is unpleasant to remember, I push them from my mind. Even now, the idea of making friends leaves me uneasy. The only friend who has stuck over the years is Frances, and that's because she never lets me down.

But Frances knows nothing about babies.

So it made sense that Calvin thought being around other women would help with my anxiety about the baby. 'At least make an effort,' he said several weeks ago when the invitation to the neighbourhood book club came. 'You might like some of the women. We've been in this neighbourhood three years already.'

I shrugged and stuck the invitation on the refrigerator with a fridge magnet of a tangerine cat hanging from a tree by its claws. It read: HANG IN THERE!

I replied, 'I've got Frances.'

'You could do with a few more friends who know something about being a parent. Frances is a bit flaky, if you ask me, with her volunteer job at the animal rescue. All those dogs she brings home.'

'She's all right.' I was annoyed with his criticism. 'Why do you have to find fault with everyone?'

The book club met the first Tuesday of every month in homes comfortable with overstuffed leather sofas and chenille throws. Calvin had been right—the women were friendly and seemed genuinely interested in what I did for a living. *How rewarding to de-clutter people's lives. You must have a lot of happy customers.*

But I knew better than to be seduced by their politeness. The women in the book club had yet to invite me for a run. I'd seen them jogging down the sidewalk in their Lululemon sweatpants, pumping their arms and chatting away.

'Have you invited *them*?' Calvin asked.

'No. Anyway, I don't have time.' I had taken on more work than usual. With the booming economy, many people were getting their closets renovated.

'Well,' said Calvin, 'it's early. You've only just started to make friends.'

'I suppose.' I walked to the window. It's a pretty neighbourhood. At Christmastime the street we live on is breathtaking when the neighbours across from us light up their massive evergreen with coloured lights. At Halloween the streets are full of children running maniacally through the streets clutching orange treat bags and wearing glow-lights swinging from their necks, oblivious to the worries of life. Still, many of them will grow up with personal demons that compel them to drink too much, neglect their marriages, or ignore their parents as I've ignored my own.

Perhaps it was Calvin's encouragement to make friends, or my own feeling of loneliness that made me blurt out the news about the baby at book club one night when the subject of toilet training came up. The reactions from the women were immediate and genuine. *Oooh, that's fabulous! You must let us have a baby shower!* They cast aside their Zadie Smith novels. *Have you found an obstetrician? Are you taking folic acid?*

Thanks to Calvin I knew about folic acid, dutifully popping the maternity vitamin he laid out for me every morning along with my herbal tea. I'd stopped drinking alcohol, and limited my coffee and black tea. I'd also agreed to stop jogging when I reached my third trimester. As for the smoking, I'd nearly quit, allowing myself only the occasional puff when the pressure was overwhelming.

If I'd been honest I would have told them how frightened I was of children—not just the experience of childbirth (which terrified me so much I stopped breathing when I imagined it), but the way small children clung to their mothers, howling with displeasure. The city was full of self-absorbed toddlers being strolled around the malls in their expensive Bugaboo strollers with Cheerios crowding their mouths. You couldn't enter a restaurant these days without tripping over a row of high chairs.

I was as careful as I'd been in Concord High to pretend I had no worries, smiling with false serenity when the Book Club women patted my belly. *Yes, it's very exciting. We can't wait.*

Calvin pointed out, 'There are books that might make you feel better.'

I visited the parenting section in Chapters, picking up *The Girlfriends' Guide to Pregnancy* and *What to Expect When You're Expecting*. The first book discussed topics such as hair dyeing and sex during pregnancy (both yeses); the second gave a month-by-month description of the growing fetus. My baby was now the size of an apple. It had taste buds; its heartbeat was developed enough for detection. Soon the baby would react to loud, sudden sounds with a startle reflex, and be able to grasp things with its tiny hands.

What you couldn't learn in a book, I wanted to tell Calvin, was how to feel like a natural mother instead of an imposter who had to remind herself to say hello to children. Other than Ryan, small children made me awkward. I watched how other people reacted to them, bending down to the child's level and smiling not just with their mouths but also with their eyes. According to the latest book I was reading, *Authentic Happiness*, the skin around the corners of the eyes crinkled in an authentic smile—as opposed to a Pan American smile, a term coined after the perfunctory smiles of the flight attendants in advertisements.

I felt very Pan American about the whole experience. One night I caught Calvin staring at me across the dining table. 'What?'

'Nothing,' he replied quickly.

'Do you think I'm eating too much? I've hardly gained any weight.'

'Of course not. Why would you think that? Anyway, you can expect to get a little bigger so don't get freaked out about it.'

'That's supposed to make me feel good?'

'I'm just saying that you can expect to gain a bit of weight. It's unhealthy not to.'

'You don't have to worry, Calvin. I won't starve the baby.'

'Why do you have to turn everything I say against me? I don't understand why you're so paranoid.'

'I'm sorry.' I stood and cleared his dish. I wasn't paranoid, just scared. 'I'm feeling irritable today.'

'It's the hormones. I can clear the table. Sit.' He took my wrist and pulled me back into my chair. 'Once the baby's here you won't have much time for anything.' He balanced my dish on top of his and headed to the kitchen. 'Do you remember Sanjay from my hockey team?' he yelled from the kitchen. 'His wife is having a baby. Due this summer. They want a boy. It's the first grandchild for both families.'

'You don't always get what you want.'

'I know, I know—as long as it's healthy.' He came back to the table. I pushed the empty salad bowl toward him.

'That can wait.' He ignored the bowl and sat in the chair beside me, reaching for my foot. 'How about a massage?'

'Certain acupuncture points in the foot bring on early labour,' I pointed out.

'Yeah?'

'You're the one who's done most of the reading.' But I'd been reading more than I admitted, staring at the drawings of babies—they looked like tadpoles. My tadpole had already begun taking over my body with its cravings for oranges and distaste for red meat. There were constant reminders that my life had irrevocably been given over to another human being—even more so than it had with marriage which I had, in truth, always considered to be somewhat impermanent. A contract that could be broken with a single conversation if either party wished, a few clothes shoved into a Samsonite, the house key left on the kitchen counter where it would be easily spied, its meaning gleaned.

I let my foot rest in Calvin's warm hand. 'I'm sorry I'm so difficult lately. I don't know what's wrong with me.'

Calvin squeezed my foot. 'You're not used to the idea of children. But look how good you are with Ryan.'

I was torn between needing Calvin and not wanting to need him. He'd been my husband for five years. I knew the pleasing angles of his face in every light, the way his body jerked before falling to sleep. I knew the scar on the bottom of his chin was from a skateboard accident at age nine, and that he favoured vanilla ice cream.

What did he see when he looked at me? Often he noticed my moodiness—

'You're so far away,' he'd complained more than once.

'Am I?'

'There's always something … so distant. As though you're trying to guard yourself.'

'Against you?'

'No, that isn't it. Although it does seem like you're never quite sure of me.'

Another time he came up behind me as I was washing my face in the bathroom sink and put his arms around my waist. I shuddered involuntarily.

'Relax.' He laughed uneasily. 'You'd think I was a stranger.'

'Don't be silly.' I unstiffened my shoulders. We stared at each other unblinkingly in the mirror, silent with all the words we were avoiding.

So many moments like this—him moving closer and me fighting the urge to withdraw.

I knew my remoteness saddened him.

With his optimism about the future, he reminded me that I was less than ready for this child. But were my fears based on practical matters, such as being overwhelmed by the tasks of caring for a baby? Or did I fear that I wouldn't grow to love the baby as I was supposed to, with my tendency to push people away before they got to know me?

What a messed-up excuse for a wife and mother-to-be I was.

My work has always been a panacea. There is satisfaction in creating order out of chaos, even if I'm not addressing the problems in my own life. Last month I designed a closet for a woman who lives in the tony neighbourhood of Elbow Park. Hers was a character house, beautiful with its original wood detailing. But the tiny closet was a challenge, with unfinished walls that had clearly been ignored in the home's last renovation.

'How're you doing in here?' The woman brought me ice water in a heavy tumbler.

'Fine.' I stepped out of the closet. 'It's going to take a bit of figuring, but I can manage.'

'You came highly recommended by my friend Sally Whittaker. Do you remember her? The house on Sifton Boulevard?

I nod politely even though I usually don't pay too much attention to the clients' names. It's their closets I remember. But that day I was uncharacteristically perturbed with my client, with her sleek ponytail and designer jeans. I wanted her to be snotty, demanding that belt racks be included in the cost. To ask for built-in laundry hampers after I had already plugged the measurements into my computer program.

Instead she said sweetly, 'Your own closet must be immaculate. I seem to be a bit of a hoarder, I'm afraid.'

'Oh.' I looked at the clothes folded into neat piles on the cheap wire shelves. 'You're not bad at all.'

'You think so?' She smiled, pleased with herself. 'My husband thinks I have too many clothes. I'll tell him you said I'm not so bad.'

I pulled out my tape measure so she'd know I was ready to end the conversation. 'I'll bring the finished blueprints downstairs when I'm done.'

'Of course.' She walked out of the bedroom and down the hallway.

I measured the height and width of each wall, determined to get the most hanging space for my client. The unfinished walls reminded me of the attic in our old rental house in Edmonton, whose rickety stairs were hidden behind a small door in the upstairs hallway. My mother was always cautioning us: *Keep off those stairs if you know what's good for you.*

One time I talked Dorothea into climbing up to the attic. 'Don't be a baby,' I said, 'there's nothing to be afraid of.' She followed me reluctantly, bracing herself with a hand against the wall as we climbed the hidden steps.

'It's too dark,' Dorothea moaned. 'What if there are mice?'

The small attic window let in a narrow beam of light that revealed the attic's contents. The attic was forbidden not only because of its decrepit stairs, but also for the treasures it contained—my mother's knee-length ivory wedding dress, worn for my parents' civil ceremony in 1965. Baby clothes folded and stored in neatly labelled cardboard boxes. A case, which I knew held my mother's antique porcelain dolls, sat chalky with dust on the coarse wooden floor planks. The dolls were the main reason she kept us from the attic, not wanting to risk their fragile painted heads, which she'd meticulously cared for.

'Be quiet.' I put my hand on Dorothea's shoulder to keep her from leaving.

My mother, noticing the house had gone silent, began calling for us, her footsteps creaking below us. Her voice was annoyed at first, then frightened, and I realized with a sinking feeling we would be punished for causing her to worry. Between the rows of clothing and stacks of boxes, we sat numb with fear. Dorothea slipped her small hand around mine and I allowed her to take it, understanding it was I who would get most of the blame.

Our mother finally opened the door to the attic stairs. By then our eyes had become adjusted to the light, and so we saw her before she saw us. She reached the top of the stairs, squinting and reaching for the light string. 'If you girls are in here, you'd better speak up.'

Dorothea let out a snivel and I slapped her knee, hissing, 'Ssshhh!'

My mother inched toward us in her house slippers until she was standing over us. 'What on earth are you thinking? You know how dangerous these stairs are! I expected more from you, Zoe.'

I waited for her to jerk me up by the arm angrily, but for once she did nothing, glaring as though not sure what to do with us. She pulled the light string so the room was dark again and marched back downstairs. 'Come along then. As long as you're all right.'

Dorothea's hand relaxed around mine. I pushed away from her, embarrassed.

'Go off and play,' my mother said when we stepped into the warm, bright kitchen. 'And don't leave your sister to play alone.' She stood at the sink with her back to us rinsing soap foam from a plate.

I nodded, relieved to be getting off so easily. But I was bothered, too, that I always had to be responsible for Dorothea.

That was years ago, why was I still provoked by the typical grudges of an eldest child? And why did I keep returning to scenes of my mother scolding me, as though she'd never once been kind?

I got back to work on the Elbow Park closet. The walls would need drywall, mudding and paint. I would ask my contractor to install new chrome hanging rods, mahogany shelves and drawers. I'd forgotten to ask if my client wanted a lingerie drawer. I decided to include one; she could always use it for the scarves that hung in a bunch on the back of her closet door. She would be pleased with my thoroughness.

I looked around at the suit jackets hanging from the existing rods—no doubt belonging to the good-looking husband smiling out from the black-and-white studio portraits that stood on the dresser. I wondered if he screwed around on business trips, telling himself he wasn't hurting anyone. Perhaps the woman drank too much—a late-afternoon glass of wine to deal with the noisy children who clamoured home after school, hungry for food and attention. I could tell by the blue and pink bedrooms there were two children, a boy and a girl—what would be called *a million-dollar family.*

Perhaps the woman followed the glass of wine with another to make up for the fact that her husband stayed holed up in his study all evening while she wandered about the house straightening pillows and wondering how they were ever going to get things back on track.

Or perhaps they were all, generally, happy. Who was I to wish them unhappiness? Could I not imagine a marriage that wasn't weighed down by separation? In my own life I was able to compartmentalize not only shoes and handbags, but my growing unrest.

In my mind I'd built a closet of my own. The top shelf held a box filled with my failings, past and present. I had yet to take it down and peer inside, to draw a mental line between then and now. I sat down on the floor of the Elbow Park closet, my computer cradled in my lap. I was so tired. For the first time, the idea of designing yet another closet fatigued me. I was tempted to put away my measuring tape and shut down my laptop without saving my blueprints. The hanging shirts brushed the back of my neck, reminding me I had work to do, but the act of reorganizing clothes felt suddenly, overwhelmingly, trivial. My mind went completely blank for several moments as my usual enthusiasm for work drained away, leaving an unsettling void. What was it that I cared about? It seemed my entire adult life had been about keeping things tidy instead of resolved.

That afternoon I'd experienced a transformation of sorts. At the time the shift went unrecognized. If I'd had to articulate my feelings I would have simply said I was exhausted. But really, I was experiencing the type of utter weariness that can only precede change. If I'd paid attention, I would have predicted a shake-up leading to my current state, where, for the first time, I was questioning whether my stubborn independence truly served me well. I hadn't yet acknowledged it, but I'd come to a crossroads where decisions had to be made. With the baby coming, there was an even greater sense that I needed to figure things out.

And what had I done with these whispers of feeling? Nothing but search out Kyle, looking for distraction the way a child tosses one toy aside for a shinier trifle.

'Are you all right?' The woman had come upstairs so quietly I hadn't heard her footsteps on the hardwood floor.

'It's the baby,' I said stupidly.

She stared at me, uncomprehending.

'I mean, I'm pregnant.'

'Oh,' she said, relieved. 'I was worried for a moment.'

I held out shiny brochures to change the subject. 'I forgot to ask about shoe fences. Do you want them?'

She waved the brochures away with the confidence of someone with money. 'Whatever you think. I'm sure you'll do a good job.'

I nodded and looked around me. Soon their small, cluttered space would be filled with blouses and slacks hanging from expensive wooden hangers. Designer purses and satchels would sit properly in their plastic dividers. Shoes would peek out from tilted shelves, easy to access. I decided to include complimentary lilac sachets in the drawers, a small kindness I could easily provide. Whatever problems this family might or might not have, for once someone's problems wouldn't be because of me.

Fourteen

'Nice of you to finally join us.' Dorothea uses her fingers to tear shreds of meat off a chicken leg for Ryan. The entire family is sitting around the table eating a late lunch of Kentucky Fried Chicken and coleslaw from paper plates. Someone has set down plastic utensils at my place.

'I got held up by a train,' I lie. The truth is, I went for a drive after leaving Marnie's house. I hadn't wanted to stay at Marnie's, but I hadn't wanted to come home either. I'd driven out to the edge of town where the giant Home Hardware warehouse stood. I pulled over to the side of the road, guilt rising like bile in my throat. What was I doing, playing around with my life so carelessly? I thought about what Marnie had said, about karma. Was it inevitable that I would return to Kyle? Was I still seeking closure? (God, I hate that term.) Or worst of all, was I still in love with him in spite of how many times he'd let me down?

'Come here,' Kyle had said last night in his living room, putting down an unfinished panel titled *Modern Fairy Tale*, a woman leaning over two sleeping children, peeling an apple with a paring knife that pierced her thumb. Although the image was only roughly sketched in charcoal the woman's eyes were clearly mad, in a style I'd come to see was not so much modern Gothic but modern suffering. Was this how Kyle got through life, by creating images that hinted at his own deep loneliness rather than dealing with it? If I stayed with him, would that be my unhappiness, too? Calvin had his shortcomings, certainly, but apathy wasn't one of them.

I'd stood up from the stool where I'd been perched uncomfortably and had gone to Kyle without hesitation. No matter that he fondled my breasts through my blouse in front of the window whose curtains were wide open.

As I stared at the Home Hardware I wondered what the impulse to destroy everything I'd worked so hard for was based on. Certainly there was physical desire—I only had to think about the muscular curve of Kyle's naked back as he turned away to reach for his beer bottle from the bedside table. Last week Calvin had sat in front of the computer, shirtless and wearing baggy boxer shorts, comparing the price of gas lawnmowers. 'We should replace the old one before summer comes,' he said. 'There's a sale at Canadian Tire.' It was unfair to compare the two, I knew that unequivocally. And if I did compare, I would find Calvin superior in many ways—he was funnier, more handsome, responsible. Certainly he was less prone to selfishness.

When I left Concord all those years ago it had been to leave behind the mess I'd created. I'd promised myself I would do better and I had, creating a life that is successful—

This thing with Kyle has caught me in a sandstorm. The wider I try to open my eyes, the more I'm blinded. I thought, at first, that his e-mails were a harmless flirtation, the sort of thing that gives a jolt of excitement in the middle of a dull day. I'm not naive enough to think we are special, or even different, from those other couples who reconnect midway through life. Worst of all, I'm pulled away from what's most important—my family, my coming home, mending the rift with Calvin.

Dorothea pulls the chicken bucket toward her. 'No one expected you on time anyway.'

'Who wants coleslaw?' my mother asks in the pleasant tone she uses when she wants to keep the conversation from sliding into an argument.

I put my plastic fork down. 'I've come all the way here, like you asked. What more do you want?'

'Girls,' my mother warns.

'Why bother coming home if it's only to help pack? You'll just go back to Calgary, and the next time we'll hear from you is to say you can't make it home for Easter.' Dorothea pulls her hair reflexively over her deformed ear.

I ignore her, wishing I were back in Calgary. My father sits hunched over his plate, oblivious to the barbs of our conversation. I suspect he turns his hearing aid off when he wants a break. 'Dad.' I wave my hand in front of his face.

'Eh?' He looks up, startled.

'I was only seeing if you were listening.'

'Don't be smart.' My mother scrapes coleslaw into the garburator.

I push away from the table. 'I'll finish sorting through the basement. I might as well be of some use while I'm here.'

'Oh Zoe.' She crams the paper plate into the trash. 'You're always so touchy.'

I go downstairs, grateful to soon be leaving Concord and all the family drama. I haven't found the right time to tell them about the baby. I can't bear how my parents will look at me, beaming as though I've finally done something that pleases them. Or how Dorothea will scowl at the news, no doubt angered that my parents are pleased with me when they should be unforgiving of my years of absence.

In my mother's basement sewing room are neatly labelled boxes of sewing supplies—seam rippers, clothing patterns and the spools of coloured thread she used to make our Halloween costumes and Sunday school outfits. She'd made our graduation dresses, too—frothy creations with oversized shoulder pads. I close the boxes and label them for Goodwill.

'Your mother might need those things.' My father appears suddenly in the doorway.

'I doubt it. She's having a hard time giving things away, you shouldn't encourage her.' I step past him to the rumpus room.

He follows. 'You shouldn't be so hard on her. It's difficult to move, after so many years in the same house.'

'You know how she is—she always needs to be in control.' I eye the bookshelf to see what I can toss, aware that my own need for order makes me a hypocrite.

'I want to keep the true-crime books. The rest, I don't care about.'

'You don't seriously want to keep them, Dad? They're so trashy.' I touch the row of paper spines. Then I feel guilty—if these books give my father pleasure, who am I to question?

'When I came to Canada I missed my parents. I could only talk with them now and then by telephone.' He stands beside the bookshelf, his hands hanging awkwardly at his sides. He seems smaller and uncertain, as though his power has been neutered by age. As a child I'd been half afraid of his size, wanting to feel his arms around me but also frightened by the strength of his squeeze.

'I know, Dad. But Mom and I—we don't see eye to eye.' I pull a packing box toward me and load it with paperbacks. My mother's yoga books and magazines crisp with age go into the box. I leave the true-crime books on the shelf.

'You could visit more often.'

'I'm trying.' I busy myself packing away the board games we used to play on snowy afternoons. 'But it always ends the same way, with both of us being disappointed. Maybe it's better if I don't spend too much time. Not to mention how Dorothea and I don't get along—that can't be easy on you and Mom.'

'No.' He bends to lift a heavy stack of *Good Housekeeping* magazines.

'Watch your heart.' I take them from him. If Calvin saw me lifting he would worry, too.

'I'm not dead yet.' He walks to the fake stone fireplace and points to the mounted rainbow trout on the mantel. 'Remember when we caught this?' He smiles, shaking his head at the memory.

I smile back. When I was a teenager the two of us went trout fishing on Bitter Lake, bobbing uneasily in the boat and busying ourselves with our rods so we wouldn't have to make conversation. Now and then my father reached over to help with my line. Suddenly I felt a tug. My father got up quickly to help me reel in the fish, his strong arms encircling mine. His breath had been warm and sweet with the coffee he'd drunk from his Thermos. 'Thatta girl!' he said excitedly. We pulled the fish in together, watching with amazement as it twitched angrily at the bottom of the boat.

The fish has stood mounted on a piece of driftwood for over twenty years, its mouth gaping open in shock. 'What do you want to do with it?' I ask.

'You probably want to take it home to show Calvin.' He picks it up by its base. 'You can't buy something like this.'

'That's for sure.' I can imagine Calvin's face when he sees it. I'll place it on our own mantel for a laugh. I pick up a ceramic ashtray filled with paper clips and dump it in a garbage bag. 'I know Mom made this ashtray but you guys really need to downsize.'

'Are you happy with Calvin?' my father asks, wrapping the base of the mounted fish carefully in newspaper. He looks around for a box.

'He's a good guy, don't worry.'

'You two thinking about having kids? Your mother told me not to ask.'

'She thinks a baby will make me happy?'

'I dunno what she thinks. Maybe we shouldn't assume you want to have a family.' He sighs and places the wrapped fish on the lacquered tree-trunk coffee table. 'You young women don't always want children nowadays.'

I hand him the lava lamp from the bookshelf. 'Hold on to this for a moment.'

'You know,' he says, taking the lamp, 'I may not make it more than a few years. My condition is serious.'

'Come on, Dad. Don't talk like that. The medication's working well.'

'Even so. One day it will be too late.' He pauses. 'Your mother and I—we know we made mistakes. But we didn't make all the mistakes.'

'What's that supposed to mean?'

'I'm not laying blame. I'm just saying it isn't easy raising children. You try your best but it's never good enough. I worry most for your mother. She keeps things inside. Things you don't know about.'

I sit back on my heels. 'What do you mean?'

'I probably shouldn't say.' He hesitates, but then continues. 'She had another baby, before you. It died a few days after birth. Something was wrong but the doctors couldn't tell us what. Then you were born and I thought that would be enough.'

'Does Dorothea know?'

'Your mother never wanted to talk about it.' He clears his throat. 'It's not that she wasn't happy with you girls. Maybe she was depressed. Who knows? Maybe it was my fault. I expected her to get on with things, especially when she got pregnant again.'

'Was it a boy or a girl?'

'A girl. We called her Zoe, too.' He cradles the lava lamp. The tears of the lamp have long ago dried up. 'I guess this is for the trash?'

I sink onto my heels. Another Zoe? I'm a *replacement*? My mother has told me many times, only half joking, that my colic nearly drove her insane. All I know of my infanthood are tales of drudgery—the cloth diapers that had to be rinsed in the toilet, the milk fever that blistered my mother's nipples, the incessant squalling. Had she expected a sweet, calm baby to restore equilibrium? Was I a disappointment from the beginning?

'I've upset you.' My father looks remorseful.

'It's okay. I guess it's better knowing. It helps me understand.' All those years my mother seemed so frantic and angry. Now that I'm pregnant I can already begin to appreciate the difficult nature of motherhood. She would have been despondent over the loss of the first Zoe, and burdened by the brutal demands of the baby she'd had to replace her. I'd always thought of Mom as merely having the type of nature that could never be satisfied, a trait I feared I'd inherited.

'You can talk to her about it if you need to. Even if you don't believe it, your mother just wants you to be happy.' He hands me the lava lamp and heads for the stairs, his work-callused hands holding on carefully to the railing.

I'm older by nearly a dozen years than my mother was when she conceived me. She'd had three pregnancies by the time she was thirty. Her husband had been mostly absent, busy with work outside the home, leaving her to bear the strain of parenthood on her own. But they'd both tried hard with what they'd been given. Where is the sense in bringing up painful memories now?

Tired, I open an unlabelled box my mother had dragged out of the utility room earlier, saying, 'This one's full of your old things, make sure you take it with you when you leave.' In an envelope is a yellowed newspaper clipping of my birthday horoscope from the last summer of high school, folded carefully as though it held some sort of clue:

If July 8 is your birthday you may not be religious in the orthodox sense, but you are spiritual. You have recently learned many lessons, and have grown in ways that cannot be measured in the material sense. Before summer is over, scenario will highlight much transformation.

A bland, generic horoscope that barely hinted at the way my life would shift course.

In the box there are loose photographs taken with my old Kodak Brownie—a photograph of my girlfriends at Pathfinders camp, their skinny legs sticking out from stiff blue skirt folds. There are yearbooks and school concert programs from Concord High. I pull out a piece of white terry cloth, unaware what it is until I unfold it to see the loonie-sized spot of blood.

And then I remember—

When I was sixteen I got my first period, discovering it in the bathroom before gym class, staring in horror at the crimson bloom in the crotch of my cotton panties. I tied my jacket around my waist before I went out to the running track so no one would see the stain spreading to my white terry-cloth shorts. Kara ran past me, her hair woven into neat French braids.

The gym teacher quickly blew her whistle when she saw me. 'Zoe Lemonopolous, take your jacket off before you trip!'

I untied the jacket and placed it on the bleachers, being careful not to bend over—although I could tell by Kara's sneer that I'd already been found out.

When I got home my mother took one look at the jacket tied around my blue jeans. 'You started your period.'

'How can you tell?' I pulled the door to the basement closed so Dorothea, who was downstairs watching television, wouldn't hear, but once my mother brought out the box of sanitary napkins and yakked to her friends on the telephone, there was no way it would remain a secret.

'I'm not an idiot.' She threaded a dishtowel through the oven-door handle. 'Come with me,' she said. 'I expected this sooner.' She pulled down a box of sanitary pads from her bedroom closet and an old-fashioned sanitary belt. My mother had attended every sex-education class at the high school, where the health nurse had laid all the modern products on a desk—tampons, self-adhesive napkins. How could she give me a belt that would show its bumpy clasps through my clothes?

I backed away. 'Can't you get some of the newer kind?'

'Don't fuss.' My mother slid the box toward me. 'I'll get some next time I go shopping.'

'That's not until Monday.'

'You can wear these for now. For God's sake, Zoe, quit being so dramatic. I'll put the box under the bathroom sink. You need to change regularly. Try not to leak. You don't want any accidents.'

What did regularly mean? Once a day? Every hour? I wasn't sure how there could possibly be a leak from the pad that sat wadded between my legs like a mattress.

'It's okay to have an accident now and then,' my mother said in front of my father the next morning at the breakfast table. 'You can't prevent every one.' If I thought I was humiliated then, it was nothing compared to the mortification I felt later that day when my soiled shorts, which I'd hidden in my locker, were hung on the basketball net for everyone to see during the Remembrance Day assembly.

I'd heard the girls conspiring in the hallway before the assembly.

'What's going on?' I asked, curious.

'Nothing.' Kara looked me in the eye while the other girls looked away, suddenly busy with their locker combinations. I smiled dumbly as we all filed into the gymnasium, not sure what was going on until I looked up to see my shorts hanging lopsidedly from the basketball net.

Kids milled around the net—

'Ew, gross! Is that blood?'

'Whose shorts are those?'

'For God's sake.' The gym teacher poked at the shorts with her floor-hockey stick. 'Have some respect.'

The principal saw what was going on and made a commotion of pulling a bench over and jabbing uselessly at the shorts with his pen. The gym teacher finally got the shorts unhooked and they fell to the ground.

'Whose are these?' The principal pointed at the shorts, demanding to know. 'Can't we do anything around here without having a sideshow?'

Kara finally spoke up. 'We don't know who those shorts belong to.' The gym was filling with students.

The principal picked up the shorts with the pen, looking helplessly at the gym teacher, and then glaring at us before marching away. 'Take your seats, girls. No more nonsense, you hear?'

We were herded to the assembly, where I sat far away from the other girls. My brain throbbed with questions. Who had seen the shorts? Had *Kyle* seen them? I knew it must have been Kara—who else knew my locker combination?

A war veteran shuffled to the podium to recite the poem we'd memorized in English class:

In Flanders fields the poppies blow
Between the crosses, row on row ...

I recited the poem mechanically without paying attention to the words. I had tried so hard to be a good friend for nearly three years, yet this was how they still treated me. The red velvet poppy pinned to my blouse had come loose. I pushed against the poppy with my hand, puncturing my palm. I barely flinched. What hurt me more was the betrayal of my friends, who sat together whispering, not daring to turn and meet my eyes. Only Marnie turned once to look sympathetically.

I cycled home after school and then lay on my bed, my abdomen cramping with rage and expelled blood. My mother checked my forehead the next day when I complained of a fever: 'You're fine, no need to miss school.'

For days I ignored Kara and the girls.

I'm busy, I said when they invited me home after school.

What's wrong? They were sweet to me, no doubt understanding they'd gone too far.

I've got homework.

But after two weeks I relented. I knew if I didn't, their sweetness would turn to meanness. They would whisper when I approached in the school hallway. They would enlist kids from other groups who were eager to please Kara, making it feel as though the entire school was against me. The girls would come up with a humiliating nickname that would stick through the rest of high school. I would be known as *Feta Farter*, or the like. My mother's favourite expression kept coming back to me: *Keep your friends close, and your enemies closer.*

I knew she was right.

So when Kara offered to show me her newly decorated bedroom—an apology of sorts—I gave in. In spite of my anger, I was curious about the Gunnersons' house renovation. Whereas our bungalow was decorated in dull shades of oatmeal and avocado down to the matching refrigerator and stove, the Gunnersons' home was modern in style. This was obvious from the red shag carpet, the foil wallpaper and the Scandinavian steel-and-glass furniture they'd bought from a store in Edmonton. Kara even had a television set in her bedroom, along with a black globe chair that made me feel as though I were sitting inside a giant eight ball.

From where I sat I could watch my friends without being observed, noticing how Marnie sneaked extra helpings from the box of Dare oatmeal cookies. 'Who's the pig?' Kara peered into the empty box, narrowing her eyes at us. I ignored her. I'd decided I wasn't going to be a doormat anymore. They could force me into friendship, but for once I'd embarrass Kara as much as she'd embarrassed me. I had a plan—

I knew from watching my father insulate the garage that fibreglass was painfully itchy. Unable to help myself from touching the soft pink insulation, I'd gotten it in my eyes and had to have it rinsed out by my exasperated mother.

I took a small piece of fibreglass with me to Kara's house the day she invited me back. The girls were in the kitchen rummaging for potato chips while I rubbed the fibreglass in the soft cotton crotch of her underwear.

'What were you doing in my bedroom?' Kara asked accusingly.

I'd shrugged innocently. 'Nothing. Don't be so suspicious.'

Today, as I examine my gym shorts, the stain is much smaller than I remembered. What cruel things girls do to each other. But I'd been mean, too—watching Kara squirm in the seat of her desk. The glass fibres caused so much pain she'd had to see the school nurse, her hands unable to stay away from the itching in her crotch while the other kids watched with fascinated horror. She'd glared at me when she left the classroom, letting me know she suspected me. But it was an uneasy glare, one that told me she'd be more careful about crossing me.

Occasionally I come across magazine articles about teenage bullying that I read with interest. I know the reasons teen girls make each other miserable—boredom, self-protection, competition, or acting out the pain of their home lives. I'm surprised to find that I feel sorry for Kara. Her father, with his dirty magazines and lewd comments, must have embarrassed her more than she let on.

I fold the shorts carefully before placing them in the trash bag.

Perhaps there is good reason to revisit old memories with an adult's eye, when you're better able to relate to the circumstances that created the hurt in the first place.

I hear my parents moving about in the kitchen upstairs. The gurgle of the coffee machine begins and the smell of coffee reaches my nose. Cupboard doors open and close. My mother is putting away clean dishes, a task she's completed thousands of times without complaint. Soon the dishes will be packed in boxes, most of them going to Dorothea's new apartment.

'Zoe,' my mother yells from upstairs. 'Coffee's ready if you want it.'

'Sure,' I yell back. I push my box aside and get up off my knees. I remember to take the Kodak Brownie for Ryan, who's playing with his toy Tonka truck at the top of the stairs. He makes a rumbling noise with his throat as the truck clatters on the landing.

Dorothea calls out to him from the kitchen. 'Take that downstairs!'

He looks down at me and notices the camera. 'What's that?'

I hold up the camera, 'It's for you.'

'Can I see?' He smiles shyly.

'Of course.' I walk up the stairs to sit on a step. He puts down his truck and sits easily beside me.

'What's it for?' He takes the Brownie in his hands. His impossibly long dark lashes lie against the perfect pink skin of his cheek, which I resist touching because I don't want to startle him. The scar from his cleft lip will bother him when he's older, just as his mother is bothered by her ear.

'For taking pictures.'

'Is it ancient?'

'Yes.' I laugh. 'Very ancient. You can keep it if you like.'

'All right.' He puts it down and picks up his truck. 'I'm going to play downstairs now.'

'Have fun.' I touch his shoulder.

He takes a step toward the basement. Too late, I spy the tape gun I'd left on one of the steps earlier. His foot lands on the pointed teeth of the gun and he yelps, pulling his foot back. The truck spills from his arms as he pitches forward, his hands grasping for the stair railing but not finding it. He falls forward, tumbling down the stairs.

A silence, then a wail. I bolt forward to reach him. My sister rushes down the steps to where he lies, face down, blood flowing from his mouth, and pushes me away. She turns him over but there's too much blood to see where he's hurt.

'It's okay.' She tries to shush him, her face ripe with fear.

'Mom!' he whimpers. 'It really hurts.'

She looks back up the stairs and sees the tape gun, then looks at me accusingly.

My parents hover at the top of the stairs. 'Oh Zoe,' my mother cries. 'How could you be so careless?'

I take my cardigan and hold it out to my sister, 'Use this.'

She bats it away. 'Get a clean towel.'

I nod robotically and rush to the bathroom to grab the pile of towels piled up on the counter.

'Not the white one.' My mother reaches for a green towel. 'Here.' She holds it gently to Ryan's face.

'I've got it.' Dorothea takes over. 'Let me see.' She takes the towel away and peers into his mouth. He opens wide, so we can all see the gash inside his mouth that will require stitches, and the chipped front tooth.

'Christ,' Dorothea mutters. 'It's a permanent tooth.'

I stand, wringing my hands. 'Calvin will fix it.'

She glares at me.

My mother says, 'She's right, honey. Calvin can fix this.'

'But it *hurts* him.' Dorothea's voice is clipped. 'Calvin can't fix that.'

Ryan has stopped crying and now sobs quietly in his mother's arms, the green towel pressed against his bleeding mouth.

'Tell your aunt to stop leaving her junk on the steps.' She hugs him. 'She should know better.'

'It was an accident, Dorothea.' My mother defends me. 'Let's not make this worse.'

I back away into the rumpus room, still holding the pile of towels. The wallpaper shows the outlines where family photos hung until recently, lighter in the places where the photos were—as though all this time the photos had covered up the fresh hope of the past.

My mother and sister discuss taking Ryan to the emergency room, leaving me out of the conversation. They decide they'll take him right away, in my parents' car. My father will stay here; the stress isn't good for him.

No one asks me to come along. When I offer to drive, my sister interrupts me: 'We're fine.'

They hurriedly pack up the car with comic books and juice for Ryan. 'We'll be back in a few hours,' my mother yells as she pulls the door shut. 'There are leftovers in the fridge.'

I sink into a kitchen chair and hear the garage door whir shut.

The kitchen table holds fresh mugs of milky coffee. I wrap my hands around a mug; it's still warm. The coffee's surface ripples and catches the overhead light. Like everything else, the coffee mug holds its own small universe of action and reaction.

After a while the coffee grows cold. I gather the mugs together wearily and take them to the sink. I wipe the coffee droplets off the table with a rag. Once I've cleaned the placemats and straightened the tea towels, I sit back down in my chair and wait. What I'm waiting for, I'm not sure.

The table gleams with Pine-Sol cleanliness. My image wavers in the shine.

The phone rings, its shrill call catching me by surprise.

Calvin is on the other end.

He is curious: 'I just got your message. Is everything all right over there?'

I tell him about Ryan's fall.

'Christ, you've got bad luck.'

'At least I was smart enough to marry a dentist. You'll be able to fix it?'

'Of course.'

I picture him sitting at his clinic desk, running his hand through his wavy dark hair as he does when he's busy. His waiting room will be noisy with end-of-day patients, reminding him that he's falling behind. But he keeps talking—

'Listen, Zoe, about the other night. I shouldn't have gotten so angry without hearing your side of the story.' He waits for my answer. Beneath the apology there is an anxious note. Perhaps he senses things have gone too far.

I stare at the telephone. My parents' wall-mounted beige telephone is so outdated it has become quaint.

I reply, 'We've both been under pressure.'

'I don't know what we're going to do about all this.'

'Me neither.' I'm not just talking about the baby. 'But this isn't something to discuss while you're at work.'

'We'll talk later, okay?' Tension shadows his voice.

I say goodbye and hang up the phone in its cradle.

I'm tired out, frayed at the ends.

I open the fridge to find a half-eaten tray of lasagna. I dig into the cold pasta with a spoon, piling it on a plate for my father who sits in his La-Z-Boy watching hockey.

'You're not gonna eat?' he asks when I bring him the heated food. 'Don't worry about Ryan. He's not the first kid to fall down the stairs.' He shovels the pasta into his mouth. 'Your sister overreacts, she'll get over it.'

'I know.' I put my hand on his shoulder. 'Can I get you anything else?'

He looks up and pats my hand. 'You're a good girl, *koukla*. I wish you knew that.'

I swallow hard. He withdraws his hand, his attention already back to the television screen. 'You wanna watch with me?'

I shake my head no. I need to get out of this house with its mingling smells of Pine-Sol and reheated hamburger. The air is too warm, my forehead is clammy. Suddenly I feel claustrophobic.

I get my purse and jacket from the hook at the back door. I go to my father, turning the handle of my purse anxiously in my hands. 'I just need a break. I'll be back soon.'

He turns his body to face me, surprised. 'Where are you going?'

'Just out for a while, nowhere special,' I reassure him, pointing him back to his channel.

I pull my car out of the driveway, not admitting to myself where I'm going. *Just a drive*, I tell myself. My car passes houses with dead brown lawns and children's bicycles left cold and forgotten all winter. The sun is starting to go down, the lawns lit by street lights.

I pull onto Main Street, where banners boast: SMALL-TOWN PRIDE.

With its bank, grocery, hairdresser, florist and stationery shop, Main Street had been the centre of our lives. I'd never questioned that everything I needed could be found within this short stretch of road. In the past year a Money Mart has appeared, taking over the Parthenon Pizza and Steak House to my father's deep disappointment. The Golden Dragon is still here, its neon red sign advertising: LUNCH SMORGAS-BORD $8.99.

I think about Calvin's call, and how a few short days ago I would've been relieved by his apology. Now I'm just confused. North of Main Street is the older section of town where duplexes and small war-time houses stand in rows. The giant cross of the Grace Lutheran Church comes into view, reminding me of my transgressions.

On Christmas Eve in Jasper I went by myself to the Lutheran Church holiday service. 'I guess you don't want to come,' I'd said to Calvin.

'You can repent for the both of us,' he joked.

In the Jasper church, the minister brought the congregation to its feet with a sweeping motion of his hands—*Praise to the Lord!* The congregation replied with a vigorous rendition of 'Joy to the World'. I closed my song-book and looked around at the people dressed in suits and satin dresses. A young boy of about two broke away and ran down the aisle to be chased by his father. I couldn't imagine myself as someone's mother. I'd be the type of parent who whisked the child away quickly, embarrassed by the public attention.

The children who marched down the aisle in a re-creation of the nativity story, wearing yarn beards, were solemn with the responsibility of remembering their lines. A few pews ahead of me, three bored teenagers slouched over their songbooks. With their youthful arrogance and lack of life experience, how could they anticipate the foolish teenage moments that might play out for years ahead?

Calvin poked fun when I returned to the hotel: 'Did you see God in church? Was he dressed up for Christmas?'

'Don't be a smartass.' I'd swatted him playfully with my church program.

But if there *was* a God, it appeared to be a chaotic, disorganized God who let things unfold like a game of checkers, mostly by chance.

I shake my head at the memory of Calvin's good-natured teasing. How had we moved so quickly from easy conversation to uncomfortable silences over the telephone?

I drive past the Concord Times building and a row of apartment houses to reach my stopping place—

Kyle answers the door, smiling to see me. 'What's wrong?' he asks when he sees my face, his smile turning to a puzzled frown.

'I'm sorry, I shouldn't have come.' I stand on the front stoop shivering. 'I don't know why I'm here.'

He steps back so I can come in. 'Is it the baby?'

I shake my head.

'Then what?'

'Nothing. I don't know.' I'm chagrined to find myself crying.

He takes me by the arm, alarmed, and leads me to the sofa. My boots are still on, leaving damp marks on the hardwood floor. He notices the marks, but says, 'Leave your boots on, it doesn't matter.'

'I don't know why I'm such a wreck. I was okay until now.' I take a deep breath and tell him about Ryan. 'I just can't seem to do anything right.'

'It was an accident. Your sister's always been hard on you. It's all that old stuff coming up again—you've got to put it in perspective.' He squeezes my arm. 'Listen, I'll make you some tea.'

He gets up and putters in the kitchen. The door to a pink bedroom is ajar. Unlike the rest of the bungalow, the room is frilly with curtains and lace-edged pillows. I'm moved by the pink walls and can imagine Kyle straining to reach the ceiling with a paintbrush. When he comes back he's brought a tray. A spoon rests neatly beside a white mug and a pot of sugar.

I put the mug to my mouth and drink. His domesticity surprises me.

'Feeling better?'

'I'm sorry to come here and cry all over you. I've made a mess of your floor.' I stand, still wearing my jacket and boots. 'I should get out of your hair.'

'Stay. Melanie's with her grandmother tonight.'

I stand, wavering.

'I told you I wanted to see you again, didn't I?' He pulls me back down to sit on the sofa. 'Besides'—he grins—'I've got something to show you.' Without waiting for my reply he moves toward a stack of canvases leaning against a wall and flips through them. 'I found this yesterday. It might make you laugh.'

He holds up a painting of me as a teenager, dressed in my navy windbreaker and leaning against my old ten-speed bicycle at the entrance to the Garden City Trailer Court. The Chinese pavement unwinds in the background.

'That's amazing.' I smile for the first time since Ryan's fall.

'I painted it a long time ago. I see the mistakes now. But I like how it looks as if you're getting ready to ride away from town.'

'I remember you wanted to get away even more.'

He gives me a lopsided smile. 'Things happen.'

'Yes. They do.' I lean forward and trace the Chinese pavement with my finger. 'I can't believe you were thinking about me.'

He sits beside me on the sofa. We stare for a long time at the painting. He says, 'It must have been hard for you to come around to the trailer court back then. With Ray and his drinking.'

'I wanted to be with you,' I say simply.

'And now?'

'Don't ask me that.' I change the subject. 'This painting—it's not bleak like the others.'

'You were never depressing to me. You were always the one person I could talk to about the stuff going on at home. You always made things easier.'

'Well, it's nice to be thought of like that. I don't think anyone else would think of me as easy.'

He laughs. 'I didn't say you were easy. But you were never a source of grief.'

I tell myself I should leave.

But I find myself unburdening: 'I never thought you cared that much, actually. That I could disappear and it wouldn't matter that you'd ever known me.' I laugh, embarrassed. 'Anyway. That's what I believed.'

'Why would you think that?'

I pause for a moment, not wanting to be dramatic. 'I guess it's what I've believed about everyone, if you want to know the truth. Like I could vanish and it wouldn't be that devastating to anyone, not really.'

'Your parents would be devastated. Even your sister.'

I scoff. 'Sure.'

'Come on.' He moves closer. 'You know it's not true.' He places his hands on my shoulders. 'Besides, it would bother me.'

And then he is pulling me toward him, his hands pushing aside my winter parka so that we're on the hardwood floor feeling everything—the gaps in the boards that pull at my bare skin, the panties pushed aside to eager fingers, the softness of his hair against my cheek. But most of all, the lack of control that causes him to whisper an admission: 'Why can't I stop thinking about you?'

We suspend movement to stare at each other.

'You feel it too.' He says it as though it's a statement, not a question.

He holds my eyes with his own, unblinking.

Nothing can change this, he seems to be saying. We could make room for everything that stands in our way, it could all work out somehow. Years of emotions held tight crack open, rushing through me like water to a crevice. A train rumbles past outside. I place my hand on his chest to feel the pounding of his heart, and finally understand that I've come here to see if I'd ever really mattered.

And now that I have my answer, does it make any difference?

Fifteen

By grade eleven it's not only the girls who've betrayed me—Kyle has started keeping his distance, too. For days he's been avoiding me, moving quickly down the hall while I follow behind him trying to catch up. He doesn't invite me to the Kinsmen Beer Fest that all the kids have been talking about for days.

Marnie offers to take me instead.

I tell my mother I'm babysitting for the Mahood family. She cuts an onion into quarters for the frying pan. 'I can drive you.'

'Don't worry. It's close.' I rush out the door before she can insist.

Marnie and Cam are waiting at the end of Maple Crescent in his truck. We'll go together to the Beer Fest, which is at the community centre two miles from town.

The waitress at the Beer Fest turns a blind eye to the fact that no one is of drinking age when she takes our order for draft beer. I sit at the table beside Marnie, trying to catch Kyle's attention.

When he gets up from the table, I follow and say, 'Getting a drink?'

He shoves his fingers in the pockets of his jeans and looks down at the floor while he walks. 'I'm not waiting for the waitress to bring my beer.'

'You seem strange tonight.' My voice is accusing even though I mean it to sound casual.

He keeps his eyes down. 'I'm all right.' He puts his money on the counter for the bartender.

I place my money beside his, embarrassed by the sight of my ragged cuticles. 'You can talk to me, you know? We're friends.' I've imagined this conversation many times, hoping there's still a chance for us.

He pushes his money closer to the bartender impatiently. 'I guess you heard about Kara and me.'

'Oh?' I look at the table where Kara sits with her chin resting on her hands, laughing at someone's joke. 'How long?'

'How long what?'

'How long have you been seeing each other?' My mind searches back for signs I've missed. Have they all known? Of course they have.

'Couple of weeks.' He takes a drag of his cigarette, avoiding my eyes.

The bartender slides two mugs of beer across the counter.

I force a smile and swallow a bitter mouthful. Even Marnie has kept quiet. I bite my thumbnail. The other girls have smooth, crescent-shaped fingernails while mine are gnawed at the edges. Of all the girls in Concord, he's chosen Kara—when it seemed he didn't even like her. I know the reason, of course. It's the same reason everyone wants Kara—because she doesn't really want them. She's like a model in a glossy fashion magazine: unattainable and therefore special. She's more interested in putting people down and then pulling them up so they're grateful. I want to scream, *You must be kidding!* But I've let Kara do the same many times myself, and will only be looked on with pity if I tell Kyle it won't last.

I push my way back to the table through the crowd of people lined up behind me at the bar.

'What's wrong?' Marnie asks.

'You knew about them?' I motion toward Kara and Kyle.

'I should've told you, I guess.'

'What difference would it make?' My friends are slamming their mugs of fresh beer on the table in a game of Captain Puff, trying to guzzle the beer before it froths over onto the tabletop. Kara's arm is on Kyle's shoulder now, her fingers curling a piece of hair at the back of his neck. I know that Kyle's hair is softer than a girl's and smells of lemon shampoo. I know how long he spends in front of the mirror with his blow-dryer and Goody hairbrush, making sure his hair lies against his neck in a straight line, and now Kara is messing it up with her careless fingers.

'I have to go.' I pick up my purse.

'You shouldn't go alone,' Marnie warns.

'I'm fine.' I leave before she can protest, tugging the heavy door open. The air is cool on my hot cheeks. When I look back Marnie has joined in the game, already forgetting about me. I'll follow the Chinese pavement home. It won't take long, and I need time to think—

'Things are good, right?' I'd asked Kyle just weeks earlier, fiddling with the passenger-door lock of his mother's Impala while we sat parked on the hill overlooking the Dumping Ground.

'Why do you ask?' he'd said, avoiding a direct answer.

I nestled my head against his shoulder and looked out at the mountain of refuse, ignoring the persistent voice that cautioned of a night such as this one, when I would know things were finally over.

For weeks Kyle and Kara have been sneaking looks at each other, causing me to cling tighter to Kyle. Who could blame him for wanting to be free of my neediness? I've been making bargains with God—*Give me back Kyle and I won't mess it up this time.*

The sound of a vehicle blowing its horn behind me interrupts my thoughts. If I were broadsided it would be an unfortunate accident—no one at fault really, just bad timing.

A Camaro whizzes past. Normally I'd be petrified to walk along a country road alone at night. There's always the threat of wild animals or dangerous strangers. But nothing could feel worse than how I feel now. September is coming. Before I know it, the final year of high school will be here, along with the usual feeling of not fitting in. My mouth fills with an unpleasant taste that has nothing to do with all the beer I've drunk. In my mind I see my friends at the Beer Fest, their heads bent over their silly game of Captain Puff so I can't see their disloyal faces. With every step I erase them, one by one.

At home, my parents' worry about money is growing worse.

They never go out anymore. My mother always seems to be dressed in a work blouse that sticks to her skin after a shift at the Parthenon. She spends her free evenings at the Singer sewing machine making dresses from Simplicity patterns as though she has somewhere to wear them. Sometimes she asks my father, 'How about a matinee?'

'You know we can't afford that.'

The final straw, according to my father, is the collection of miniature lawn gnomes my mother has placed among the boxy shrubs in front of our bungalow. Each one resembles a Disney character—Grumpy, Sleepy, Bashful—purchased from Gord's Discount Greenhouse.

'What do you think?' my mother asks, squatting to push Happy, the newest purchase, into the dirt. 'Does he look okay here?'

'Sure, whatever.' I know it's only a matter of time before my father drives up to change clothes for the evening shift—polyester dress slacks, single-stripe golf shirt, Hai Karate aftershave, good Seiko watch.

'What the hell is this?' He gets out of the car slowly and scratches his head as though he's stumbled upon a mirage.

'Don't get angry, Costa, they were on sale.'

'This is why I go to work every day?' He points at Bashful. 'What's wrong with this one? He's supposed to be retarded or what?'

'You said the house needed fixing up.'

'New siding. When we can afford it.' He takes a step closer and kicks one of the gnomes. 'You wanna keep a nice home you should keep your daughters from wearing blue jeans with rips in the knees.' He pulls his pant leg up to reveal a hole in his black sock. 'How about fixing my socks if you got so much time on your hands?'

My mother's mouth is set in a line that tells me it will be a long evening.

Later, she storms around the house picking up empty mugs and teen novels—talking to Dorothea and me only to scold us for the mess. 'This isn't a hotel,' she nags, compelling us to retreat to the rumpus room and pick fights with each other.

'You're a hog.' Dorothea grabs the TV remote control away from me.

'Am not.' I grab it back.

Eventually my mother collapses on the rumpus room sofa with exhaustion. 'Say what you will about your father, at least he works hard. If he got paid properly for his efforts, we'd be rich by now.' Dorothea and I stare at the television screen where the Six Million Dollar Man is lifting a train off the tracks with one arm.

At that moment, my father will most likely be waiting for his final customers to leave. *You people need anything else?* He will hover with his hands clasped impatiently behind his back. He'll pull the Parthenon's metal door closed when he leaves for home, yanking twice to make sure it's locked. His old Chrysler will cough to life reluctantly and he'll pull out of the alley onto Main Street. He has his eye on the new Oldsmobile Toronado, bringing home leaflets from the dealership.

'We can't afford a new car,' my mother reminds him.

'Tell me something I don't know,' he mutters, holding the edges of the leaflet with his thick, scarred thumbs. Much of the money from the Parthenon goes to my Greek grandparents, *Yiayia* and *Pappou*. 'One day,' my father promises, pointing at a sepia-toned photograph of a stern-faced couple, 'you'll see where you come from.' All I know of Greece is from the outdated calendar hanging in his den that shows two donkeys lumbering up a rocky hill with wicker baskets strapped to their backs.

For two weeks every summer my father leaves the restaurant in the care of my mother and travels to Athens on Air Canada's economy class. In Greece he eats the dishes of his childhood: fried sardines, stuffed peppers and a dish called *taramosalata* that sounds disgusting, made with fish eggs, bread and olive oil.

When he returns from his trip he's quick to point out what's wrong with Canadian life. 'No fish at the grocery?' He pokes a fork at the tuna casserole my mother places in front of him.

'The girls don't like it.'

'Hmph.' He sniffs the plate suspiciously. Then he turns his attention to me and Dorothea. 'You girls should wear dresses, those pants are for boys.'

'Thank God your father didn't marry a Greek woman,' my mother often says when he isn't around. 'Imagine what you'd have to put up with then.'

We nod in agreement. A Greek mother would make even greater outsiders of us. Our mother, with her garden gnomes and recent attempts at pottery, is not much better, though. Her misshapen ceramic bowls and pencil holders clutter our home along with our father's Greek statuettes.

One day my father comes home early in a pressed white shirt and tie.

My mother wipes soapy dishwater from her hands onto her apron. 'How did it go?' Her eyebrows are raised worriedly.

'Hard to tell.' He loosens the noose of his tie.

'You have to tell me more than that, Costa. Did the bank manager say we could have the loan? Did he want our house as collateral?'

'We'll talk about it later.' He nods toward me and Dorothea to remind her to be careful what she says in front of us. He walks through the kitchen where we are eating Velveeta melties.

'Don't walk away from me.' Her voice is shrill. 'You have a family here that needs to be supported. I need to know what's happening.'

'In Greece the women don't talk back like this.'

'Perhaps you'd like to be back in Greece.'

'It would be easier, believe me.'

'There's your goddamn complaining again. The snow! The cold! The economy! If you don't like it here then why did you come?'

'I came to make a living.'

'Well your precious Trudeau really screwed that up, didn't he?'

'Ah!' He throws his arms in the air. 'Here we go again.'

'In case you haven't noticed, we've been living on pasta and rice. The girls need new sneakers. Your dress slacks are a disgrace.'

I force myself to take a bite. If I leave *perfectly good food* on my plate, I'll never hear the end of it. The cheese has congealed into a rubbery orange mass.

My mother turns to us crossly, 'Are you girls going to play with your food all day?'

'I'm not hungry.' Dorothea's bottom lip trembles.

'Well, don't forget to rinse your plates.'

I sneak out the side door to sit beneath the Mayday tree at the back of the house. It blooms into a huge canopy each spring. This is where I go when I want to be alone with my worries. What will happen to the restaurant if my father can't make the payments? Will we have to move to the trailer court?

Dorothea appears under the branches, blocking the sunlight. 'Is Dad going to leave?'

'That's a stupid question.' I throw a piece of bark at Dorothea, who starts to cry. 'I'm going inside.'

'Can I come with you?'

'Do what you want—I don't care.'

The door to the utility room is open when we head downstairs to the rumpus room.

I stick my head inside to scan the utility room. My father's tools hang neatly from hooks—pliers, wrenches, a hammer dangling by its sharp teeth. A mountain of old paint cans stands beside the water heater. I sense movement behind the furnace and peer around to find my father pressing his knuckles into his eyes.

'Dad?' I take a step forward. 'What's wrong?'

'Nothing.' He turns away to root through his tool chest. His voice is gruff. 'You're always hanging around when you should be outside playing.'

'Are you okay?'

'I told you. Go!' He waves me outside with a pair of needle-nose pliers.

I back out of the room, stepping on Dorothea's foot.

'Ouch!' Dorothea squeals. 'Watch where you're going!'

'Watch out yourself!' I turn and run upstairs to go back outside. It's one thing to see my mother cry. She is prone to teary outbursts that end as quickly as they begin. But my *father*? I've watched him burn his forearms in the pizza oven without wincing, stopping to examine his wounds only when the pizza has been sealed in its takeout box. For my father to cry means we're in real trouble. I punch the back gate latch open and wander to the end of the alley. It's better to be outdoors, especially in warm weather when the hedge at the end of the alley is loaded down with lilac-pink bleeding-hearts whose thin-skinned chambers I tear apart. Everything seems to be falling away, first my friends, then Kyle, now my parents. I look back to make out the shallow peak of the roof of my house and see an ocean of identical tiled roofs sloping up and down like waves. At a distance, it would appear we are as happy as everyone else.

Sixteen

Loose gravel rattles beneath the car as we pull up to my grandparents' farmhouse. Dorothea and I have been here only a couple of times before, even though it's less than an hour away from Concord. Two German shepherds greet the car, barking excitedly. My grandmother rushes out to shoo them away. She marvels as Dorothea and I step onto the driveway. 'You're getting so big!' She moves toward us and smiles, but her eyes are sad.

'They're growing up,' my mother says, standing a distance away. My grandfather leans against the doorway staring at us, his red-and-black-plaid flannel shirt tucked neatly into Wranglers.

'Come, come.' Grandmother puts her arms around our shoulders, guiding us into the farmhouse and past our grandfather, who steps out of the way. Unlike my grandmother, who is round and soft, everything about my grandfather is hard, from his leather boots and metal belt buckle to his unsmiling expression.

'Hi Dad,' says my mother as she steps past him into the house.

He nods in acknowledgement.

'You remember Snowball?' My grandmother strokes the white Siamese cat that slinks between our legs. 'That cat will be nineteen years old in September.'

'Nineteen?' My mother bends down and strokes its fur. 'That hardly seems possible.'

'It's been a while,' Grandmother replies. 'You should bring the girls more often.'

'We're welcome as long as Costa doesn't come, right?' My mother pulls herself up straight. Her tailored skirt and blouse look stylish in contrast to Grandmother's wrinkled farm dress. She'd abandoned several outfits in favour of this one, asking us anxiously before we left the house: 'You can't see the run in my stocking, can you?'

'Let's not start that nonsense again, Sophie. Your father only wanted you to have the best marriage possible. Anyway, that's water under the bridge. Bring Costa if you like. It's up to you.' Her warm fleshy hand guides Dorothea and me into the kitchen where the walls are decorated with plates showing images of the Royal Family. 'You girls want a cookie?'

An oilcloth patterned with red cherry bunches covers the kitchen table. A plate of homemade gingersnaps steams in the middle of the cloth.

My grandfather sits down heavily at the head of the table, his large hands folded in front of him. He moves the plate of cookies toward us. We reach for a cookie cautiously, not arguing about who gets the largest one as we usually do. 'You girls scared of those dogs outside?'

Dorothea nods but I shake my head defiantly, feeling the need to be as tough as my mother, who holds her head high. Although I know by the way she grips her teacup that she's nervous. I realize my grandparents must also know her moods, having lived with her for more years than I've been alive.

'Good girl.' He nods approvingly, and pushes the plate closer to me.

The refrigerator breaks into a hum, then falls as silent as the rest of us. I peer down the narrow hall that leads to the bedrooms and wonder if my mother felt happy as a child growing up here. She seldom talks about her parents. Whenever I ask her for stories she changes the subject— *Why do you want to know all that? Your grandparents were busy with the farm. I played mostly with the animals. It's not a bad way to grow up, just lonely.* Did she long for a sister to laze in bed with, reading storybooks under the covers with a stolen flashlight until their mother came in to remind them that it was time for lights out?

My grandfather stares at the sugar bowl and clears his throat. 'Everything okay?' This confuses me; I'm not sure at first who he's talking to.

My mother replies too airily, 'Fine,' and sips her orange pekoe. She sets the teacup down and straightens her back, taking a deep breath. She looks at Dorothea and me as though to remind herself she's not alone, and I realize we're here because she needs us. 'We could use some help, actually. Just for a couple of months. The restaurant's been hit hard by this recession. You can't say we aren't working hard, especially Costa. He barely comes home anymore. He didn't want me to come but I insisted. What can you do in an economy like this? Everyone's hurting. Anyway, I thought you might help.' She runs a finger around the teacup's rim. There's a long silence. I hear the *tick-tock* of the kitchen clock. The drip of the kitchen sink. Dorothea's noisy chewing.

My grandfather clears his throat again. 'I figured there musta been a reason for you to finally come.'

Grandmother motions for us to get up. 'Come and see the new chicks, girls. Bring your cookies.'

I dawdle, wanting to hear their conversation. But my mother waits until the screen door claps shut.

Dorothea grins at the chicks that scamper about her feet.

'Here.' Grandmother holds a chick out to me. I refuse. The fuzzy yellow chick stares up at me but I can only wonder about what's going on inside the farmhouse.

My mother was irritable during the drive out to the farm, telling us to can it when we fought over who got to use the portable radio.

My father had been quieter than usual before we left, staring at his coffee cup as we sat around the table eating breakfast. 'You sure this is a good idea?' he asked my mother when she told Dorothea and me to get our spring jackets.

'Is there a better option?'

He sighed and got up to put his mug in the sink.

They were standing together at the sink when we came back to the kitchen in our jackets, my mother leaning against my father's chest. They broke apart when they saw us. 'You kids behave yourselves,' my father said, as though we were still babies. 'Don't make a problem for your mother, you hear?'

When we come out of the chicken coop, wiping our Sunday shoes clean of chicken droppings, my mother is waiting in the car.

'You can't stay longer?' Grandmother squeezes our shoulders as though to keep us from breaking free. Her hands are strong from years of hard work. Farm trucks on the nearby road rumble past. The air smells of pig shit. Dorothea puts her arm around Grandmother's waist.

My mother says in her no-nonsense voice, not looking at Grandmother, 'Girls, get in the car now.'

'Sophie—' Grandmother hangs on.

'I mean it, girls. Now!'

As we drive away the dogs run alongside the car, blocking the path to the gravel road. 'Don't hit them!' Dorothea pleads.

'I'll run those goddamn dogs over, I swear it,' my mother mutters. 'This whole day was a complete waste of time. Might as well get some enjoyment.'

'Why do we have to leave?' I grouse, wanting to take a closer look inside my grandparents' farmhouse. I can hardly believe the photo I saw of the young girl in pigtails smiling shyly is my mother. The house is full of interesting things: an old-fangled flip toaster and a phonograph machine, an enormous floor-model radio with fancy dials.

Dorothea sobs.

'What's your problem?' I ask crossly. 'Just shut up.' For once my mother doesn't tell me to apologize.

'So?' My father says when we get home. He is sitting outside on the top step waiting.

'I don't know why I expected anything from them.' My mother pulls off her high heels and sits beside him while Dorothea weaves a crown of wild roses from the bush.

'What did he say?'

'Just what you'd expect. We made our own bed, now lie in it.' Her voice quivers. 'You think he'd mellow over the years.'

'We'll be okay.' He stares down at his clasped hands.

My mother leans her head on his shoulder and takes the crown of roses Dorothea hands her. 'I could always work in the bank if there are any openings.' In the past, every time my mother has brought up the idea, my father has refused. *You don't need to work, Sophie. That's why I bought the restaurant.*

'Maybe.' He stands and goes indoors, leaving my mother's head to drop from his shoulder.

'Stay out here with us for a while,' she calls after him. 'It's a beautiful day—the girls don't get to see you much.' She looks down at the roses, already wilting in the heat, and cups their heads in her palm. She looks up at us and says, 'I was proud of how good you girls were today. I mean it.'

In the end she begins selling Tupperware.

Overnight our dining room is stacked high with pastel-coloured containers, Jel-Ring molds for gelatin desserts, and plastic burger presses. Several evenings a month she hosts sales parties in the homes of friends and neighbours, loading up the trunk of her station wagon with Tupperware and stacks of catalogues.

Occasionally she has the parties in our home, where she demonstrates how to 'burp' the airtight Tupperware lids while a half dozen women wearing wrap dresses and wedge sandals lean forward with anticipation. On these evenings my father doesn't come home from work until after we've all gone to bed, retrieving the cold plate of food my mother has left for him in the refrigerator.

I hear them late at night arguing about the restaurant.

'I won't let them take the house, Sophie. Quit worrying.'

'You can't just tell the bank what to do.'

'Leave it to me, okay?'

'That's been the problem.'

At times, my parents argue about my mother's spending.

'I have to look like a professional.' She has been shopping more than usual, buying clothes and shoes at the mall. She sprays her hair into a stiff helmet of Elnett while my father—always so fastidious about his appearance—often forgets to shave.

When she's not selling Tupperware, my mother is organizing her friends into a yoga class held Thursday nights in the Lutheran Church's social room.

'You're leaving again?' Dorothea whines.

'You'll be fine without me.' She pulls her elastic-waist sweatpants over her bodysuit and rummages in her purse for her car keys.

I'm glad for the silence. My mother is always moving about when she's home, and telling us what to do, never noticing how lonely I am. With my father at work and Dorothea playing by herself in her bedroom, I can lie on my bed and dream about how much better life will be when I get out of Concord. What I don't realize is how difficult it will be, years later, for us all to come together again.

Seventeen

Back at home Dorothea, Ryan and my mother have not yet returned from the hospital. The tape gun has been left on the kitchen table, its teeth pointed downward. I say hello to my father, who's distracted by the nightly news, and go to the garage to start sorting through things that need to be discarded: old bicycle helmets and ski boots that don't fit, boxes of empty liquor bottles and yards of garden hose.

I pick up a can of dried paint. It strikes me that the last time I cleaned up the garage was years ago, after the visit to my grandparents' farm, when my mother decided we'd make money by having a garage sale.

She'd been keen, saying, 'We'll make cash and get rid of junk at the same time!' She agreed to give me extra money for university if I helped. I'd already passed my high school exams easily, coming home to study each day after working at the Parthenon. 'Not bad,' my father said, when I brought him the university's scholarship letter.

When the morning of the sale arrived he left for work early, shaking his head at the lawn signs my mother had made from poster paper and tempera paint. She dragged the broken swag lamp from the rumpus room onto the driveway after he left. She told me, 'Greeks don't understand garage sales. They think we're putting our trash out for everyone to look at.' She clicked open a card table. 'We'll put hats and shoes here. And those old-fashioned white gloves—maybe someone will buy them.'

I folded a DuPont girdle for the clothing table. 'You sure you want to put your underwear out? Dad will have a conniption fit.'

'Don't worry about your father—he won't come within thirty feet of this sale. Anyway, it's not underwear. It's a support garment.' She wheeled a metal clothes hanger onto the lawn. Old parkas, shirt dresses, matching red satin bomber jackets and a denim bell-bottom jumpsuit hung from the rack. 'Maybe I should keep the jumpsuit.'

'I thought you wanted to free up closet space.'

'Well that's true.' She fingered the collar of the jumpsuit. 'I've never spent so much on an outfit.'

I didn't care if she kept it or sold it. I felt sorry for my father, who was losing his Barry Manilow and Carpenters records but didn't know it yet.

'Keep those records in a box, we'll sell them as a set.'

The neighbours peeked over the fence. 'You're having a sale?'

'Come.' My mother waved them over. 'First pick is yours.'

They shook their heads in unison. 'We don't need any more stuff.'

She turned to me enthusiastically. 'Go into the garage and get your father's golf clubs. He hasn't used them for years.' She looked back at the neighbours. 'You golf?'

I took my time inside the garage. When I hauled the clubs out I was glad to see the neighbours were gone. 'Are we done?'

'In a minute. There's still stuff in Dorothea's room to get rid of.' My mother strode purposefully back into the house, motioning for me to follow. 'Get a move on. People will be coming soon.'

'Shouldn't you wait until Dorothea gets home?' Dorothea was sleeping over at a girlfriend's house.

'Nonsense. She doesn't play with half the things in her room these days.' She opened Dorothea's closet, scooping up clothes and forgotten Barbie dolls. 'She's too old for dolls.' She peered around the room. 'Bring those stuffed animals.'

I picked up an armful of stuffed bunnies and dogs. 'She still sleeps with these.' Even though Dorothea was fifteen, she refused to let go of her favourite childhood treasures.

'Leave her a couple, then. But hurry up.' My mother was already halfway down the hall.

I flung a small spotted dog and a pink kitten onto my sister's bed.

'We're doing your room next,' my mother warned as the screen door slapped behind her.

'I'll help you in a minute, I have to pee,' I yelled, running downstairs to my bedroom to shove things under my bed, including the Mrs Beasley doll my father brought home when I was eight and that no longer talked when I pulled its string. I gathered up a stack of comic books I never read, and a ski jacket that was torn in the armpit.

'What took you so long?' My mother was sitting at the card table with a shoebox of change. 'I've already sold the records.'

'Here.' I dumped my things on the table. 'These are from my room.'

'You have to present things nicely if you're hoping to make a sale.' My mother hung the jacket on the metal rack, tucking the rip into itself. 'There, you see?'

I noticed my father's donkey calendar sitting beside a box of old cookbooks. 'Who's going to buy that?'

'People are funny. You never know what junk they'll take. If it doesn't sell, we'll hang it back on the wall. Your father won't know the difference.'

I sat at the table beside my mother on an old kitchen chair that was marked at ten dollars. My mother had forgotten we used these chairs when we had guests. Maybe she didn't care. Her tidy bun was unravelling; loose hairs sprung free from their bobby pins giving her the look of someone who was coming undone. 'Isn't this exciting?' She smiled at a group of joggers who'd slowed to take a look. 'Sport socks.' She waved a package of white socks in their direction. 'Never worn!'

'God, Mom. Stop it.' I prayed my friends wouldn't come by to smirk at my mother, who'd lost all sense of pride.

A car slowed down. An old lady stuck her head out. 'Any gardening tools?'

My mother nodded her head. 'Go to the shed,' she whispered to me sharply. 'Get me the leaf blower.'

'Are you crazy? Dad's going to kill you.'

The car pulled into the driveway.

'You let me worry about your father.' She scanned the front lawn, which was suddenly full of people. 'Free coffee!' she yelled out to the crowd. 'Great deals today!'

The garden shed smelled of dirt and turpentine. I grabbed the leaf blower from its metal hook. My father had organized the shed last summer, making sure everything had a place. He would notice the gap on the wall and there'd be another fight.

'Zoe!' my mother yelled. 'I need help out here!'

I closed the shed door and locked it behind me, noticing that the metal garbage can standing beside the back gate was stuffed with things my mother had deemed unworthy—socks with holes and half-finished crossword puzzle books. Sticking out of the can was the solar system mobile I'd made in sixth-grade science class out of construction paper and coat hangers. I'd traced and painted the nine planets carefully, arranging them in order around a yellow Styrofoam sun. 'Your parents will be proud of your work, Zoe,' my teacher had said, holding it up so the other kids could see it. The mobile had been shoved carelessly in the metal can, its planets tangled hopelessly around one another. I touched the tattered rings of Saturn, which I'd sprinkled with sparkle dust to mimic ice particles. I'd hung on to the mobile for years. It wasn't that I'd wanted to keep it forever, but the way it had been so carelessly discarded bothered me. A customary wave of anger and loss rushed over me.

I found my mother standing beside a table of kitchen gear: a hand-operated pasta maker, ceramic jars shaped as toadstools and a milkshake blender. She was showing a young couple how to use the pasta maker, her arms making exaggerated grinding motions. A kid stopped me. 'How much for the comic books?'

'Three bucks.'

'Two.'

'Fine.' I pocketed the two-dollar bill.

My mother floated by, the pasta maker in her arms. 'Make sure you keep an eye on the money.'

I nodded and stepped back. There was no sense confronting my mother about the mobile now. People swarmed like flies around our cast-aways. My father's bowling shoes were gone, Dorothea's Barbie collection, the entire set of Nancy Drews my mother had put out at the last minute, saying, 'You girls never read them.' I noticed a woman walking past with a green striped vase my parents had received as a wedding present. It was true my father never liked the vase, but still.

I checked the shoebox. So far we'd made one hundred and twelve dollars.

Once the flush of new money was gone my mother would realize she'd sold expensive items for a fraction of their worth. Dorothea and my father would be furious. Dorothea would tear open her closet, asking, *Why didn't you stop her?* and not believing I'd done my best.

My father would be too angry to speak. He would storm out of the house and back to the restaurant, leaving us alone with my mother, who'd act as though nothing was wrong. *I don't know why everyone's so angry,* she would huff. *I was only trying to help.*

'Zoe!' she called me. 'Look who's here!'

Marnie and her father were getting out of their truck. Marnie walked up to me reluctantly. 'You made any money yet?'

'A bit.' Since the Beer Fest, I'd kept my distance from the girls.

Marnie's dad prodded the clothes on the rack with his tobacco-stained fingers. 'You see anything you like?' he asked Marnie. 'You're always complaining you need new clothes.'

'Not those.' She gave him a dirty look. He wandered over to the card table and picked up a set of mismatched towels.

'I told him not to stop,' Marnie said. 'But he saw the crowd.' She ran a hand over a satin bomber jacket. 'You think your mother will get rid of this tacky thing?' We burst out laughing.

'At least *your* stuff isn't getting sold for peanuts.'

'True.' She nodded and fingered my parka. 'You guys doing okay at the restaurant?'

'Sure. Why do you ask?'

'No reason.'

'Did someone say something?'

'Relax. Why are you getting so worked up?'

'I'm not.' I straightened the clothes hanging from the rack and changed the subject. 'Have you decided what you're doing when September comes?' I was being mean—I knew Marnie's father couldn't afford to send her to university, and her marks weren't good enough for a scholarship. Marnie worked hard babysitting on the weekends just to buy her own clothes and school supplies.

'I dunno.' She dropped the parka sleeve. 'Maybe I'll work at the bank.'

'I guess Cam will still be around.'

She glowered at me. 'He's not someone I want to be with forever, you know?'

I nodded. Everything about Cam smacked of desperation—the way he picked at his acne scars, the dingy flannel jacket he wore no matter what the weather, the rank smell of his truck's upholstery. I imagined him fifteen years older, still driving wrecks and scrounging for cash.

'Do you know what Kyle's doing in the fall?' Marnie arched her eyebrows as though daring me to ask for more information. I'd kept myself busy working at the restaurant to avoid them all, especially Kara, who acted as if she'd done nothing wrong, wearing Kyle's athletic jacket with the sleeves rolled up like I used to.

I knew the high school art teacher wanted Kyle to attend college. Twice his paintings had been entered in the Klondike Days art competition in Edmonton. He had what the art teacher called *a natural gift*. I was at the trailer when Kyle told his mother about the first competition. 'No one else from the school qualified.'

'No one else is stupid enough to waste their time,' Ray had remarked. 'This is what you get,' he told Mrs Lipinski, 'for encouraging him to be a sissy.'

I asked Marnie, 'What about art school?'

With an air of knowledge she informed me, 'Ray wants him to learn a trade. He says art school's a waste of time.'

'What about Kara?'

'She's going to the university in Victoria. She's leaving as soon as school's over to spend the summer with her aunt.'

'Good.'

I looked away to see my mother counting the money in the shoebox. A man and his two sons were carting off the kitchen chairs. In my fantasies Kyle lived in the trailer with Ray and the rest of his family, pining for escape in the same way I'd pined for him. He was stuck in Concord despite his promise to leave. In my fantasies I was the happy one—the one who got away. I touched the two-dollar bill in my pocket. There would be more money to add to my savings once the sale was over. Suddenly I was anxious to help my mother sell as much as we could.

'Your dad's leaving, you'd better go.' I gestured toward Marnie's father, who was packing the towels and a frying pan into his truck. 'You want the parka or what?'

'Nah.' Marnie headed toward the truck. 'I've got enough junk. See you Monday.'

'See you.' I pushed the parka back onto the rack. I'd hoped my friends wouldn't find out about the sale. Now Marnie would tell them all about it.

A woman in flowered capri pants circled the golf clubs. 'How much for these?'

I saw my mother shoving bills into her bra. She was too far away to hear. 'Not for sale.'

The woman pointed to Dorothea's bicycle, which Dorothea had left propped against the house. 'That?'

'No.' I took the bike by its handles. 'That's definitely not for sale.'

The lady looked disappointed until she spied the denim jumpsuit. 'Ah.' She held it against herself. 'This looks like my size.'

I balanced the bike against my hip while I took the woman's money, and then wheeled it to the back shed. I went inside the house and looked through the picture window at the pieces of our lives strewn across the lawn like debris from a summer storm. I kept my eye on the shoebox sitting on the card table. When it was all over I would accept my money guiltily. My father and sister would blame me as much as they blamed my mother. I'd show Dorothea where the bicycle was hidden: 'Don't say I didn't look out for you.'

What was it with my mother, always pushing our family to the edge of argument?

Nothing had worked out as I'd hoped it would when I stood at the window the night we moved to Concord, looking out at the clear night sky with my father's hand placed reassuringly on my shoulder.

Tonight, as I move old paint cans to a corner of the garage beside the empty liquor bottles, I'm grateful for the deflection of work. The metal paint-can handles cut into my palms and I'm glad for the pain because it distracts me from thoughts of Kyle.

I pull hoses down from hooks on the wall, looping them in coils. I drag an old step-ladder over to the high shelves and step on it to reach boxes nearly hidden from view, sorting through rusty nails, cement glue and spare fuses. Whatever needs sorting or piling, I'm eager to do it. I'll work until my arms give out from the strain to avoid thinking about the events of the past few days.

My father opens the door to the garage. 'You okay? You don't want anything to eat?'

'I'm fine,' I tell him, not pausing.

'Okay,' he replies doubtfully, and closes the door.

I could go and sit with him, watching the evening news while he leans back in his La-Z-Boy commenting on the stock market or a suicide bombing in Iraq. I could nod to show I'm listening, never letting on about my own brewing drama.

The garage door whirs, telling me Dorothea and my mother are finally home with Ryan.

I step aside to let my mother park the car and wait for them to get out. I see that in spite of the heavy bleeding earlier, only a small bandage covers Ryan's lip.

My mother opens the door to the house and hangs her purse on a hook. She takes off her coat and sighs. 'What a day.'

Dorothea ushers Ryan into the living room. I follow them.

My father stands up and looks Ryan over. 'You all right, son?'

Ryan nods and reaches shyly for Dorothea. She unzips his jacket and tells my father, 'He was very brave today, Dad. You would've been proud of him.'

We sit on the sofa with its plastic-covered headrests. I'm still not used to being allowed in this room—as teenagers we were sent downstairs to the rumpus room to entertain ourselves. I resist the urge to rub out the impression my foot makes in the plush carpet. I tell myself it's just being in this particular room that makes me feel unwelcome.

Dorothea turns to look at me, surprising me with her conciliatory tone. 'It's going to be fine, you don't need to worry.'

Relief floods over me. 'Good. That's terrific.' It seems possible we're talking on two levels. The first is about Ryan, of course. A second, perhaps, is that Dorothea has calmed down enough not to hold a grudge.

My mother, witnessing our attempts at peace, jumps into the conversation. 'Things always seem worse at first, girls. I remember one time when you two were playing outside in wintertime and Zoe licked the metal porch railing and got her tongue stuck. She must've been about six. It was one of the coldest days of the years. I panicked and pulled her off the railing but the skin of her tongue came off, too. The screams were so loud I was sure the neighbours were going to come to see what was happening. Anyway, you got over it quickly. Kids always do.'

I reassure Dorothea, 'I've called Calvin about the tooth. He says it'll be no problem to fix.'

My mother nods, pleased.

'Good,' Dorothea replies. She stands up abruptly and takes Ryan by the hand. 'We need to get you to bed, kid.'

He rubs his eyes, which are drooping from the long day.

Dorothea heads down the hall with Ryan, disappearing into herself, just as she had when she was a teenager and sensed we were getting too close.

'They'll both be fine,' my mother tells me. Her eyes seem to sink more deeply in their sockets. No doubt she's tired, not just from packing but from the tension of the week. 'We'll get back to things tomorrow.'

I nod. 'There's not much left to do. I've cleared most of the garage. We're in good shape.' I'm talking, of course, about all the packing and sorting I've accomplished since I got back from Kyle's.

But as for the rest of it?

We'll never entirely get back to where we started.

Eighteen

In 1985, the summer of graduation, my classmates and I set off on separate roads, unaware of the ruts that lie ahead—

Most of the kids plan to stay in Concord. Many hope to work in the bank as Marnie will, or at the Home Hardware warehouse stocking shelves. Some of the boys will leave Concord to work on the oil rigs, coming home on their days off to sit in the Parthenon Lounge and plug coins into the slot machines until their money is gone.

My mother has agreed to let me go to the graduation party at Janice's cabin at Bitter Lake. She warned me—*No drugs. No drinking. Got it?*

I nodded vigorously, not sure why I was so interested in going to the party when I'd been so determined to avoid my friends. I was just weeks from moving away for university—perhaps I wanted to see them all one last time to prove to myself I didn't need them anymore. Or perhaps I wanted them to see that I was going to make something of myself. I didn't give it much thought, although in the back of my mind I knew I wanted to see Kyle again before I left.

When I pull up with Marnie and Cam everyone is gathered around a campfire. Someone has put stereo speakers in the flatbed of a truck. 'Do You Really Want to Hurt Me?' by Boy George is playing so loudly the ground appears to be shaking.

Someone yells, 'Turn that gay shit off!'

Someone shouts back, 'Go fuck yourself!'

'You want a beer?' Cam pulls a case of Labatt's from behind the seat.

We nod. The party mood is frantic. For weeks all talk has been about the last day of school and prom dates. Now we've finally reached the long-awaited evening, and things seem to be ending and beginning at the same time.

Cam puts his arm around Marnie, who pulls away. 'What's the problem?' he asks.

'Nothing. Why do you have to be so possessive?' She looks at me as though to say, *Help me get rid of him.* I ignore her. *Life is a game of dominoes,* I think—the slightest push toward the person you want and all you ever get is the motion of *away*. Besides, what has Marnie done to help me lately?

I've watched her with the other girls, discussing graduation dresses. My dress was made by my mother on her sewing machine: it's Woolworth's faux satin bought on sale—the cheap slippery fabric nothing like the crisp taffeta I'd asked for.

'C'mon, you guys.' Kyle sees us and motions toward the lake. 'We're going swimming.' He's dressed in cut-offs and a sweatshirt, smiling. This is the first time he's acknowledged me in ages.

By the time we make our way down the narrow path to the lake it's twilight—a dusky light that compels the girls to curl their toes protectively against algae they cannot see to avoid. 'Last one in is a rotten egg!' Kara pulls off her T-shirt to uncover a bikini that reveals pale bands of flesh. I tug at the bottom of my new one-piece swimsuit—until now I'd felt good about how I looked.

The lake is cool for June. Every now and then one of the girls screams and jumps into a boy's arms, frightened by the sensation that comes from touching something foreign at the bottom of the lake with her bare feet: a piece of soda-bottle glass rubbed smooth by sand and water; or a shred of discarded clothing that wraps around the ankle like the unwelcome flicker of a tongue. 'It's just seaweed for Christ's sake,' the boy says. But he smiles when he says it, happy to cradle a pretty girl in his young muscled arms.

In the middle of the lake is a small island called Lou's Point, named for the fellow who operates Local Lou's Weekender and Gas. The kids hang out all summer at Local Lou's, eating soft-serve ice cream and guzzling cans of vodka-spiked root beer, grinding cigarettes into the dirt with the toes of their sneakers. They smoke their cigarettes behind the store, careful not to get caught smoking too close to the gas pumps.

'Race you to the Point,' yells Kyle, who's already up to his waist.

'Don't be crazy,' Janice yells back. 'You could drown out there.' We girls are always the ones to remind the boys of perils—the stomach cramps, the beer they've drunk, the scolding they'll get if the rural police catch them swimming past curfew. The boys' arms are a fury of front-crawl strokes designed to impress the girls left behind in a state of nervousness trying to keep track of the heads bobbing away from them.

Without the boys to keep us warm we grow goose bumps and huddle together to stop shivering.

'Crazy fools. They can't even see where they're swimming to,' murmurs Marnie.

Kara sighs as though Marnie's anxiety bores her. 'The Point isn't even a quarter of a mile away. A blind person could make it. If they drown it's not our fault. I'm getting out before the cold makes me sick.' She wades through the shallow water, her nipples pressing against the small triangles of her bikini. The moonlight shows the curves of her legs and arms. If she knew Kyle had brushed up beside me with his bare arm while she'd been preoccupied with re-tying her bikini top, she'd be furious. '*Oops.*' He'd grinned mischievously.

We follow Kara, dragging our legs slowly through the water until we reach our pile of beach towels and shorts. The narrow path back to the cabin is overgrown with branches that need to be swatted aside. The ground beneath our sneakers is uneven from the tree roots that braid together to form a lumpy pathway. 'Isn't there an easier way?' Kara complains.

Janice holds the branches, handing them to Kara as she passes. 'I know where I'm going.'

Kara releases the branches, which strike my face. 'Sorry, I didn't know you were behind me.'

'It's okay.' I rub my cheek, fuming.

'Wait up!' The boys have made their way back from Lou's Point to join us on the path, arguing over who won the race. *You pussy, you didn't come close to winning. You didn't even go all the way to the island, jerk-off.* They grab one another in headlocks. Kara and Janice hurry ahead to the cabin.

Kyle taps me on the shoulder. 'What's the rush?'

I stop and turn around. 'I need to change into something dry.'

He smiles at the T-shirt sticking to my damp skin. 'I see that.'

'You're going to get me in trouble.' I cross my arms in front of my chest. 'Anyway, half the time you don't know I'm alive.'

He sighs. 'I don't want to fight.'

'What do you want from me, then?' I've studied hard and worked extra hours at the restaurant to make money for university so I can escape the weight of him.

He reaches out to touch my neck, his hand cool against my skin. 'Don't be like that.'

I tell myself to step back. I've struggled to get over him—have been embarrassed and even frightened by the strength of my feelings. The panic of losing him has been replaced with a steady, burning desire to keep going on, a survival instinct I wasn't aware I had. Instead I stand still, waiting for what happens next.

'I'm sorry.' He traces the ridge of my collarbone with his thumb. 'I've just been thinking about you a lot.'

I flinch at his touch. 'What about Kara?'

'She's leaving soon for university. What does she care?'

'Well, don't start something you don't intend to finish.' I sound bold but inside I'm shaking with anticipation. How many times have I stared at his back in the school hallway, waiting for him to turn around and admit that he missed me, that I was worth missing?

'You're so mad.' Kyle pushes harder on my collarbone. 'We've always been friends.'

I stare at him. *Friends?* Friends don't break your heart. Or ignore you for months. If I could talk I would tell him this. Instead I stand mutely—all my resolve to forget about him dissolving under the pressure of his thumb. As much as I hate him, I still love him.

The night air breezes against my damp T-shirt and I shiver with cold.

'You all right?' He pulls me toward him by my waist.

I rest my head against his soft cotton sweatshirt. 'Fine.'

We both stand, unmoving. My fingers, wrapped around his waist, feel the soft fuzz of his lower back. In spite of the recent months there is a sense of belonging I feel only with him.

His breath is warm against my forehead. In the background Bitter Lake slaps against the shore, an ebb and flow that will continue long after we're all gone. Back at the party kids are acting as though nothing will change, as though a few short years from now it will still be possible to come together as a group. My mother has always said, *Make the most of your high school years, they go by so quickly.* To me, the high school years have been a slow trickle.

Kara calls out, a disembodied voice from far ahead in the bushes. 'Kyle, are you coming?'

'You're being summoned,' I say sarcastically, refusing to be the first one to move away.

'I'll talk to you later, okay?' He steps back.

I watch as he hurries ahead, aware that I'm holding my breath like I always do when I'm trying not to panic.

Nineteen

In the weeks since the graduation party, things have gotten better at home.

The restaurant has been busier, so my father is less uptight about money. When he comes home after work he doesn't disappear into his den, sighing whenever Dorothea or I bother him. We stand behind him at his desk, leaning close while he shows us how to handle the stamps from his collection—carefully, with tweezers.

Even my mother seems content, finally able to order the new dining table she's wanted since we moved to Concord. 'Like I always say,' she says excitedly when the heavy oak table gets carried out of the Sears delivery truck, 'things do get better if you believe they can.'

She takes me shopping, to the new West Edmonton Mall for university clothes, telling me, 'You can't go crazy, of course, but pick out a few things you like.' We eat teriyaki chicken in the food court, clumsily with chopsticks. 'It's going to be okay,' she says, smiling sadly. I'm confused, thinking she's talking about the chopsticks, until I realize she's talking about my move to university.

She shakes her head. 'Look at me going on like this. You'll have a great time away from home.'

I nod, quiet. I've been desperate to escape Concord, never realizing I might still be lonely in a new place.

As though reading my thoughts she reaches over and touches my arm. 'Don't worry, it'll be an adventure. You can come home to visit anytime you like, you know that.'

After lunch we drive to the University of Alberta's Rutherford Library for the orientation tour, standing in the middle of the grand hall like country bumpkins, craning our necks to stare at the high ceiling. The university is a maze of buildings, gymnasiums and theatres. We trail the tour guide as she rattles off statistics. There are thirty thousand students at the University of Alberta, more than three times the population of Concord. Suddenly there's a change of class and the pathways are congested with students rushing to their next lecture.

Even though I'm uneasy about being alone at university, I'm grateful for the opportunity to be free of Kyle for good. For days I've jumped at the sound of the phone, rushing to pick it up in case it's him. My mother has grown curious: 'Who are you waiting for?'

'No one,' I lie.

On the August long weekend my parents rent a cabin at Bitter Lake. Usually I can't bear the drive, watching a carsick Dorothea clutch her plastic pail. But I'm happy to get out of town and away from the hot restaurant. I help pack the cooler with ice to keep the egg-salad sandwiches and tins of Fanta cool for our lunch. On the drive to the lake I squeeze low in my seat to read my book, half listening to my mother's chatter and my father's occasional replies. The back of the car is a refuge.

The cabin is set far back from the lake, separated from the beach by a busy road and rows of newer cabins. There's a weedy patch of perennials planted long ago by someone who'd cared about the yard. My mother is pleased with the cabin, calling it *charming*. She unloads groceries into the old Maytag refrigerator and wipes the toast crumbs left behind by previous tenants. 'You girls are lucky, I never had a vacation like this.' She moves the radio dial to find a country station, whistling while she works. The kitchen curtains are yellowed with age and hang loosely from their rings.

We sit on the rotting front porch reading Archie comics and cracking sunflower seeds open with our teeth. Dorothea sits beside me, her legs tan and long. She has begun to develop breasts. The sun beats down on our bare heads prompting my mother to yell out the window, 'Girls, get some sun hats on!'

We grin at each other and roll our eyes, going inside to flop on the worn sofa and thumb through faded magazines. My farther paces about the small cabin, opening windows to let in *some goddamn air!*

'You girls go outside,' my mother says. 'You don't need to be indoors on a day like this.'

Dorothea and I have already been down to the lake to stick our toes in the murky water, drawing them out quickly, slick with scum. It's a bad year for algae bloom. Birds walk on mats of rotting vegetation floating in the lake. Dead whitefish bob bloated and dull in the water, reminding us to stay out or risk swimmer's itch.

'We'll go back down to the beach,' I tell my mother. I wait for Dorothea to come out of the bathroom, her cheeks brightly rouged. Next year she'll be in high school.

We stand at the main road waiting to cross. A rust-pocked Chevy truck filled with shirtless boys wearing baseball caps slows down and someone yells, 'Hey ladies!' A whistle, then another, as the boys wait for our reaction. I recognize them as boys who dropped out of last year's senior class—Dallas Smith and the odd-looking Laverty brothers, Marcus and Jonas, whose eyelashes are so blond they appear to be missing.

'Ignore them,' I tell Dorothea, looking straight ahead. 'They're bad news.'

She giggles, glancing back in their direction.

'They'll never leave us alone if you lead them on,' I say knowingly. Dorothea follows as I cross the road and push through the bushes that lead to the lake.

The beach is thick with sandflies that buzz about our heads. 'What a waste,' I say, looking out at the forbidden lake. Dorothea nods and picks up a branch, dragging it through the sand while we walk. Farther east down the beach are the lakefront cabins where the Gunnersons have their vacation home. No doubt Kara is sunning herself on the wraparound deck, perhaps with Janice or Marnie lying nearby. Kyle works weekends at the Sport Swap, so he'll be back in Concord. I strain my eyes but cannot see through the large evergreens that conceal the lakefront cabins from the rest of us.

We walk farther, reaching the pier. Local Lou's convenience store is a half block away, a modern white structure that rises gleaming in our view. There's always something to see at Local Lou's, where the window posters advertise gas and fireworks.

'Let's get some ketchup chips,' I say, fingering the dollar bills in the pocket of my cut-offs.

Dorothea drops her stick and walks faster, happy to be included.

At the corner store we also fill small plastic bags with penny candy—blue whales, cinnamon hearts, hot rocks that fizzle on our tongues. The store is cooled by a large whirring fan that makes us forget, for a moment, that we can't jump in the lake to cool down.

The store is full of teenagers buying cigarettes and Freezie pops. Outside, trucks wheel around the parking lot. Gas fumes make waves in the hot summer air. Dorothea stares out the window at the commotion, sucking on a candy sour.

'Don't gawk,' I tell her.

The bell over the door clangs and Kara walks in with her mother. I sneak to the back of the store where the canned goods are stacked in tidy rows.

'What're you doing?' Dorothea follows, pulling at the back of my tank top.

'Nothing. Never mind.' I loiter beside the cans of Spam and Chef Boyardee. To my chagrin I hear Kara's footsteps grow near until she's standing in the same aisle staring at me.

She looks surprised. 'What're you doing here?'

'Just hanging around,' I mumble, embarrassed by my ratty cut-offs. If I wanted to be mean, I could tell her about Kyle. Who would be humiliated then?

Kara looks amused. Then she notices Dorothea. 'I see you brought your kid sister.' She smirks at Dorothea, whose rouged cheeks are red as a clown's.

'I had to bring her,' I say meanly, ignoring how Dorothea's face crumples with hurt.

Mrs Gunnerson comes around the corner into our aisle, her clogs clicking on the floor. 'Zoe, hello! So nice to see you! You girls are out for the day?'

'We're renting a cabin.'

'Wonderful.' She looks at Kara, who looks away. She reaches for a giant can of Libby's baked beans. 'Ready, honey?'

Kara nods and follows her mother to the till. Mrs Gunnerson pays for the beans with a crisp twenty-dollar bill, slipping the change into a sleek wallet. She waves at us, her wrists clinking with expensive bangles.

I wave back, not expecting an invitation.

Two summers ago, when Kara and I were still friends, I'd stayed at the Gunnersons' cabin for an entire week. One afternoon her parents took us out on their boat, *Lady Luck*. We'd jumped off the side of the boat, screaming at the cold water and hugging each other to stay warm. When the sun began to set we'd motored back to the Gunnersons' cabin. Mr Gunnerson doused his firepit with a container of gasoline causing an enormous flare that made him jump back with a tense laugh. Mrs Gunnerson showed us how to press melted marshmallows and chocolate squares between graham crackers. *You'll always remember these times, girls.* She'd smiled at how we gobbled the gooey treats.

'What's your deal?' I snap at Dorothea, who sulks, pressing her fingers into her empty candy bag to get the last grains of sugar.

She ignores me and walks out the door.

The Chevy truck with the boys we'd seen earlier pulls up to the store.

One of the Laverty brothers calls to us: 'You girls want a lift?'

I pull Dorothea by the arm. 'We're fine.'

'You're not my mother.' She shakes my hand away and steps toward the truck.

'Get in.' Dallas sticks his head out the driver's-side window.

'Don't be stupid,' I plead with Dorothea, blocking her way.

She steps around me and places her foot on the running board. Dallas gets out and helps her in. She moves away from me, to sit near the passenger window, on Jonas's lap. Resigned, I crawl in beside Dorothea to sit in the middle, on Marcus's lap, furious at my sister. Marcus grabs me around the waist as the truck bumps up and down over potholes.

'You're friends with Kara Gunnerson,' Dallas says.

'Sort of.' I think of the way Kara smirked at us.

'She's one hot piece of ass.' Dallas grins and turns the truck toward the highway. He nods toward Dorothea. 'This your sister?'

'She's not in high school yet, so don't get any ideas.'

Dorothea glares.

'Don't worry,' Dallas says smoothly, taking a joint from Jonas and sucking in the smoke. 'We'll take good care of you both.'

Jonas chuckles. His arm is squeezed under Dorothea's breasts, his arm hair pale as a girl's.

My bare legs are hot against Marcus's jeans. I grab the lip of the dashboard and lean forward so I don't have to feel him pressing against me. The stick shift digs into my thigh. A bag of Cheezies and a pack of Zig-Zag rolling papers shift back and forth on the dash. The air inside the truck smells of pot and sweat.

'You girls up for a joyride?' Dallas pushes down on the stick shift without waiting for an answer. The truck whines into high gear. The speedometer needle surges all the way to the right. Dallas pulls the truck past a station wagon, fishtailing wildly.

We're coming up to a blind bend in the road. I lose my grip on the dashboard, sliding back into Marcus's lap. The bag of Cheezies flies across the dash, loose orange nuggets tumbling to the floor.

Dallas pulls the truck into the opposite lane of the highway in a game of chicken. If there's a car coming around the bend, it won't see us until it's too late.

'Stop!' I say, panicked. 'You could kill us.'

If my parents could see us now they'd be speechless at the sight of

Dorothea and me sitting inches from the windshield, nothing to hold us back but the arms of these stoned boys. For all the times Dorothea has blamed me for getting us into trouble, it'll be her fault if we smash through the glass of the windshield.

'I've got you.' Marcus pulls me tightly to him. His Saint Christopher medallion scratches the back of my neck. I grip his leg with my left hand instinctually, reaching out with my right to hold on to Dorothea's leg.

We make it around the corner, the truck squealing out of the bend. The boys hoot at our good luck, high-fiving one another and laughing. I glance at Dorothea, whose face is bright with excitement. The golf course whips past, then the Vacation Bible School where Seventh-day Adventists send their children for day camp. A school bus carrying kids slows down at the turnoff to the school. Dallas pulls the truck past the bus without slowing down. 'Fifty bucks for each kid you hit!' Jonas shouts.

Dorothea giggles, then catches me frowning at her. She looks away, annoyed.

'Shit, I forgot to get gas,' Dallas complains, glancing at the gas gauge. He scowls and pulls the truck around to head back to Bitter Lake. 'Fun's over, kids.'

We get to the gas station and tumble out of the truck crunching the Cheezies with our shoes.

'That's enough,' I say to Dorothea, 'We're not getting back in with them.' I wait for her to step down from the running board reluctantly. She stands away from me, still angry.

'You're crazy,' I tell her as we walk away, ignoring the boys' protests. 'You know that?'

'As if you care what happens to me.' She stomps through the brush, leaving me to hurry after her.

My mother puts down her knitting when we get in. 'Where did you two go? Do you have any idea how long you've been gone?'

'We were just hanging around.' I can't stay in the room with all three of them staring at me disapprovingly. 'I'm going to take a shower.'

'Well, don't use all the water. Let your sister in so she can wash up.' My mother pushes her glasses atop her head. 'You've missed dinner.'

I pull a towel around my chest as Dorothea stomps into the bathroom. I wait outside the bathroom door in my towel for her to finish washing.

'Why are you so sulky?' My mother eyes me suspiciously.

'No reason.'

Dorothea comes out of the bathroom. 'I'm done.'

'Finally.' I push past her and lock the bathroom door. For the next two nights Dorothea and I are expected to share a double bed and spend all our time together. My mother is always reminding me, *You may not care for your sister now, but soon she'll grow up and it will be a blessing to have someone besides your parents to count on.*

No matter what she says, I don't see how we'll ever care enough to count on each other. And judging by how easily Kyle has forgotten me again, it's clear that the only one I can count on is myself.

Twenty

Kyle and Cam show up at my parents' house a few nights after we get back from our vacation at Bitter Lake. Kyle knows my parents will be working at the restaurant like they always do on Friday nights. 'Look after each other,' my mother had said before leaving. 'We'll be late tonight.'

Dorothea and I are watching *Dynasty* in the rumpus room when the doorbell rings.

'You get it,' I say, my head comfortable on a pillow.

'No, you.'

'Fine.' I push myself off the sofa and climb the stairs, expecting to find a pair of neatly dressed churchgoers handing out religious pamphlets.

'It's you,' I say, surprised when I see Kyle. 'What're you doing here?' It's been weeks since the graduation party. I've already begun packing for university.

'I need to see you.' He leans against the door frame. 'Can you go for a drive?'

'Where to?'

'I don't know. The lake, I guess.'

Cam stands behind him, his fingers jammed into the pockets of his jeans.

'All three of us?'

'Cam can wait here for me.'

'I don't know.' My stomach twists with indecision. Cam slouches against the open door so he is already half inside.

Kyle shrugs, hurt. 'It's up to you.'

'I'll get my jacket.' I warn Cam—'You'd better behave.'

He grins. 'I'll be good, don't worry.'

I go to tell Dorothea. 'I'm going out for a bit. Cam's staying here.'

'You can't leave me here alone with him!'

'He's harmless. Just make sure he doesn't poke around.' I turn to leave, ignoring the prick of my conscience. Hadn't Marnie told me he was dodgy, and a bit too free with his hands?

On the way to Bitter Lake I ask Kyle, 'Cam won't make trouble, will he?'

'No. I promise.' He takes my hand and strokes it with his thumb. 'You don't want to go back, do you?'

'I guess not.'

We drive along the Chinese pavement in his Impala, which still carries signs of Kara, who has already moved away to Victoria—a tube of lip balm, a squeeze bottle of lotion that sits possessively on the dashboard.

I sigh.

'What's the matter?'

'Nothing. I don't know.' I twist a piece of my hair. 'What're we doing here anyway? You've got a girlfriend. It's not like you want to get back together with me.' I glance over to see his reaction.

'*Had* a girlfriend. She's gone.'

'I'll be gone soon too.'

'Why do you have to talk about that?' He stares straight ahead as he drives. I'm filled with questions. The Chinese pavement leads us past farmers' fields and the occasional farmhouse.

After a while, I speak: 'I don't want to be your second choice.'

He sighs. 'You're not. Don't make things difficult.' He slows at the turnoff to Bitter Lake and pulls over at the side of the road where a thin path leads through bush and trees to the water. He turns off the engine and lights another cigarette.

The smoke swirls through the car and makes my eyes water.

'Don't cry,' he jokes.

I smile in spite of myself and take a swig from the bottle of Jack Daniels that sits between his legs, wiping the neck of the bottle with my hand before handing it back.

He smiles. 'You don't need to wipe it. I know what you taste like.' He grows serious. 'Let's go down to the beach.'

'It's cold tonight,' I answer, doubtful. 'I have to get back to my sister.'

'Come on.' He opens his door and motions for me to follow. 'We'll keep each other warm.' He takes my hand and guides me through the prickly brush until we reach the beach, where he lays his jean jacket on the sand and pulls me down. 'You know how much I wanted to see you tonight?'

'Tell me,' I say, leaning back on my hands, flirting. The sand is cold against my palms.

'I can't explain it. Sometimes you're the only person I can talk to.'

'Is everything okay at home?' I shiver and sit up, wrapping my arms around myself. I've been so caught up in jealousy I've forgotten what life is like for Kyle at the trailer court. The air is dank with wet sand and lake water.

He shakes his head. 'It's been rough with Ray off work. He sits around all day making things shitty for the rest of us. Like it's his goddamn personal *mission* to make everyone miserable.'

'Miserable how?'

'You don't want to know.' He grabs a fistful of sand and lets it pour out of his hand.

'Of course I do.' How could he not see that I wanted to know everything about him? I might pretend he didn't matter, but I was always paying attention.

He pulls his sleeve up to reveal a huge yellowed bruise on his wrist, holding his lit cigarette close so I can see in the darkness.

'That's awful.' I place my finger gently on the bruise. 'Is that really from Ray?'

'This is what he does when I forget to buy his fucking smokes.' He looks at the black lake. 'God I hate our shitty town.'

'Doesn't your mother stop him?'

He makes a short, bitter laugh and drags on his cigarette.

'You need to get out of there. It's not good for you to live like that.'

'I'll be out of the trailer in a couple of months.'

'Where will you go?'

'I'll get a job, rent an apartment. Anything to get out of there.'

'What about art school?'

He laughs. 'You're the only one who ever thought I'd make it to art school.'

I raise his bruised wrist to my mouth, feeling grains of sand on my lips. 'No one should treat you like that.'

'Jesus,' he groans. 'Don't do that.'

I move my mouth away, afraid I've hurt him.

He laughs. 'It's not my wrist that hurts.' He guides my hand gently to the lump in his jeans. I know he'll stop if I ask. Instead, I open my hand over the warm denim of his crotch. He looks down at my hand and says in a strangled voice, 'Come closer.'

I move nearer, not considering how I should punish him for all the days I wasted waiting by the telephone. I only remember the feel of my cheek against his cotton sweatshirt the night of the graduation party, and I sense the rush of the waters of Bitter Lake, sweeping away from the shore but always returning.

I let him unzip my fly, thankful for the spotless white cotton panties my mother bought me at West Edmonton Mall instead of my old stretched-out ones, grey from getting mixed in the laundry, even though it's too dark to notice.

'Is this okay?' His fingers curl underneath my panties.

My body reacts with a tremor that startles me. 'It's okay.' I bury my face in his shoulder, shyly, thinking about the openly seductive women in Mr Gunnerson's magazines.

He takes my face between his hands in the dimness. 'I want you to look at me.'

I shake my head and turn away as he reaches out to unbutton my blouse, freeing the tiny pearl buttons from their holes. He slips his fingers inside my bra to cup my breast, my nipple springing to life under his thumb. My breathing is fast and nervous.

'It's okay,' he whispers. 'It's just me.'

He says it matter-of-factly, as though the past months haven't mattered. As though, like the lake, we're simply circling back to what is natural and certain.

He pulls out a condom from his pocket and holds it up for permission. I nod, my mind watching the scene as though someone else is making the choice for me. He tears the foil open with his teeth and pulls me beneath him.

'Here.' He takes me by my hips and slides halfway inside me. I wince at the pain.

He stops. 'You want me to keep going?'

I nod and take a deep breath. Have I been waiting all this time, only to find disappointment?

Then he is all the way inside and it's as though I've unfolded to become his perfect fit. He places his hand down low and presses in exactly the right place. His flannel shirt is soft against my skin as we rock together, locked like pieces of a puzzle. Gradually the pain gives way to a flutter, then a breathtaking ripple, and I grip his shirt overcome with gratitude.

The surging lake murmurs in my ears, telling me the cold and grit of the sand doesn't matter. Nothing matters except being here with him.

'We should get back,' I say, reluctantly moving my head off his chest. We've been lying on the beach for nearly an hour, my coat pulled over us like a blanket against the cold air.

He gets up slowly and pulls me to my feet. 'I guess you're right.' He picks up his jean jacket and shakes it clean before shrugging it on.

I sweep the sand off my jeans so my mother won't guess where I've been, but memories of this night and this beach won't be so easily brushed away. Something tells me that you step out of moments like this carefully, making sure to leave footprints you can return to find.

In the car, Kyle turns the key in the ignition and faces me—'You all right? With what we just did?'

'I think so.' My mind wanders to, and then flickers away from, the thought of my parents, who would be shocked by what just happened on the public beach. My mother has often told me, *Pregnancy and reputation are at stake for girls who put themselves in stupid positions. Remember that when you're with a boy.*

An image of Kara pops into my head. Why should I think about her? She's gone, over two thousand miles out of sight. I take the hand lotion that sits on the dashboard and shove it into the glove compartment where it won't jiggle distractingly during the drive home.

Kyle pulls the Impala onto the Chinese pavement to head back to town. He takes my hand.

'What's going to happen now?' I ask.

'I don't know ... What do you want to happen?'

'This.' I move closer toward him. A sense of expectation unfolds inside my head, much like my mother's flowering caragana bushes that bow forward to welcome me home at the end of a long shift at the Parthenon. For the first time in months I feel something that resembles joy.

He smiles without answering.

I tell myself not to analyze his silence. I need to be as confident as Kara, who understands that desperation pushes people away. In my optimistic thoughts of the future Kyle and I are *a serious couple.* There will be real jobs, a small apartment in the city and, most important, an escape from Concord. I know this is all a long way off, and I don't dare mention any of it to him. But surely we're moving toward something more.

The trees are an unbroken blur of evergreen made blacker by night. We pass scattered acreages. Here is a farmhouse, then another. Occasionally we pass a turn sign that leads to a skinny gravel road. The trees become less clustered, flickering past us one by one, only to be replaced by streetlights as we get closer to town.

Now we've reached the brightly lit Petro-Canada station whose parking lot is filled with revving trucks. The Burger Baron with its orange-and-brown castle-style exterior is hopping with high school kids drunk and stoned, craving junk food. There's a small strip mall to our right where an insurance company and a second-hand clothing store do business. Then there's the rest of the main drag: the Dairy Queen, the GM dealership and the only four-way traffic light.

Instead of leaving town, could I stay here and live with Kyle? Work at the bank with Marnie? My mind bubbles with questions.

Kyle seems only concerned with the radio dial, turning it this way and that for better reception. He catches me staring at him. 'What?' he asks.

'Nothing,' I say. 'It's nothing.'

Before we know it, we're pulling up to my house. 'Hello,' I call out at the front doorway but no one answers. The kitchen and living room are quiet except for the sound of the TV.

'Cam's shoes are gone,' says Kyle. 'He must've gotten tired of waiting.'

'Something seems wrong.' My heart beats out a caution.

'You're jumpy. Your sister's probably sleeping.' He looks at his watch. 'I should go before your parents get home.'

'Wait here.' I go down to the rumpus room and turn on the lights. It's just as it had been earlier in the evening—throw pillows tossed messily on the sofa, paperbacks on the coffee table, Dorothea's hairbrush thick with matted hair.

When I come back Kyle is waiting at the front door impatiently.

'I'll check her bedroom.' I walk slowly upstairs, motioning for Kyle to follow.

'This is crazy, I should go.'

'Not yet.'

The landing is dark but light slips out from under Dorothea's door. I knock softly and enter. Her bedside lamp is on. At first I don't see her among the pillows. She lies curled on the far side of the bed facing the wall. 'Where's Cam?' I ask.

She refuses to turn around.

I twist to look at Kyle who stands at the doorway; his face is tight and closed.

I push aside the pillows and sit on the bed touching the sleeve of Dorothea's Snow White nightgown, which is so old the sleeves only reach her elbows. 'What happened? Did he do something?'

She shudders and moves toward the wall, her shoulder blades curved away from me.

'What *happened*?' I turn to look at Kyle again, to remind him that he's responsible, too—but he's disappeared.

I turn back to Dorothea and put my arm around her. 'You have to tell me what's wrong.' I try to pull her toward me but she curls into a tighter ball. A stomach-sickening nausea replaces the joy I'd felt moments earlier. My parents will be home any minute. 'Please, Dorothea.'

'Quit touching me,' she whispers, moving closer to the wall.

The bedroom looks like it always does: clothes scattered on the floor and hair elastics littering the white dresser. The Barbie Dreamhouse is packed tidily in the corner where it has sat, unused, for years—forgotten by my mother in the garage sale. My mind protects itself from the worst-case scenario. There's no evidence anything horrible's happened. I'm pan-icking for nothing. There must be an easy answer: Cam teased her, or threatened to shut her up if she told on him for taking my father's liquor.

'You need to snap out of it,' I say firmly. But my gut flips at Dorothea's silence—she's always quick to point out what I've done wrong, threaten-ing to tell my parents at the first opportunity.

She shakes me away stubbornly.

'Fine,' I say, bewildered by the situation. 'If you won't let me help, there's nothing I can do for you.' When my parents come home they'll rush to her like they always do, turning their blaming eyes at me without first getting the story.

Then I draw my hand away and see the blood on her nightgown, con-fusing it at first with Snow White's bright red cape.

Twenty-One

The boxes are all stacked in my parents' hallway by Saturday afternoon, waiting for the movers to come on Sunday morning to take them to the Vista Grande.

On Saturday night I call Kyle. 'It's me.'

'I know who it is. You're coming over?'

'Yes. If you'd like.'

'What do *you* think?'

But now that I'm in his house the conversation is stilted. Both of us seem to understand that we need to make a decision of sorts before I leave Concord. He stands with his back to me rummaging through the refrigerator. 'I thought I had some bottled water.' He reaches behind a bag of apples and pulls out a bottle. 'I knew it was here.'

He rinses a glass tumbler. 'I don't have much to eat.'

'I'm not hungry. It's been a long day.' Dorothea has been on my case, criticizing me for weeding out photos. *Even if you don't care about these photos, Mom and Dad like to look at them.* My mother had agreed with Dorothea, taking the frames from my hands. I take a drink of water and look around Kyle's kitchen. Could I live here? My kitchen in Calgary is decorated with things I love—copper-bottomed pots and pans that hang from a ceiling rack, the hand-carved pepper mill I bought at the farmers' market, jars of dried mushrooms and colourful spices.

'Families can be a pain in the ass. But they're still family.'

'I guess so. Whatever happened to Ray?'

'My mom kicked him out years ago. I visit him sometimes in the seniors' centre. He's got no one else. Besides, he's harmless now.'

I lean back in my chair. 'He's older. That changes people.'

'Sometimes.' He sits across from me.

'Were you pleased I called?'

'Why wouldn't I be?'

'I don't know. You seem ... different.'

'It's not exactly like you're available, is it?' His voice is strangely altered. He stands up and walks to the kitchen window. I can't see his face to know what he's thinking. A dead houseplant sits on the sill.

In our house in Calgary, Calvin and I have collected our own idea of a life. There are the sleek taupe sofas bought on sale at Urban & Co.—not quite the colour we'd hoped for but neutral enough so they would do. We've set out our black-and-white travel photographs gallery-style, a single row of black-framed prints that runs across several walls, each print hanging exactly forty-two inches from the ceiling because a home-decorating magazine said to do so. 'These pictures are too low,' proclaimed my father during one of my parents' rare visits to Calgary. 'You don't worry about kids knocking them down?' We seldom had children in the house, I pointed out to him—most of our friends were childless.

'It looks funny.' My father jabbed at the picture glass with his finger. 'You two should live in a new house, you can afford it. Maybe in the southwest where you can see the mountains, like the Papas girl.' He had a friend whose daughter lived in a new house in the upscale community of Aspen Woods with walk-in closets and an oversized steam shower.

'She lives half an hour from downtown,' I reminded my father. 'How much of our lives would we lose driving?'

He moved his shoulders in a dramatic heaving motion, his hands cupped against his chest. 'Your mother and I didn't care if we pleased our parents, either.'

Kyle turns from the window. 'I'm not sure what we're doing. It doesn't matter, I guess. You're here.' He takes a step toward me and then leads me to the bedroom and pulls my sweater over my head, impatient.

I reach for him with my mouth and grip his hips with my hands. I'll pay dearly for this even if Calvin never finds out. The price of concealed infidelity, I'm starting to realize, is not so much living with guilt but living without the balm of punishment.

Is that why I keep coming back—to make myself more miserable?

When I'd visited Marnie the other day, she'd asked, 'When was the last time you were happy?'

'Happy?' I'd replied.

'Yes, happy.'

'I'm pretty balanced most of the time. Not much rattles me.'

'That doesn't answer my question.' Marnie narrowed her eyes.

'Well, that's what I call happy.' The cheerful banter of the children's television program irritated me.

'I think you don't believe you *deserve* to be happy.' Marnie scooped up her youngest son who'd toddled over to the kitchen island where we were having coffee. She smelled the crotch of his pants. 'Looks like we have a poopie, Ethan,' she proclaimed triumphantly, placing him on the kitchen floor on a duck-patterned mat.

'Quit trying to psychoanalyze me,' I said, annoyed.

She ripped the tabs of the diaper open and grimaced. 'You have to admit, you seem more than a little confused.'

'Clearly you've hit the happiness jackpot.' I turned away from the sight of Ethan's dirty diaper and his chubby legs kicking out at nothing. Still, Marnie had hit on something true. It was as though I'd been looking at my life from the outside, wondering at someone else's good luck. Calvin, the beautiful house, the job I loved, and now the baby formed a lovely picture in which I still felt like an outsider. Worst of all, my alienation had led to restless searching. And to what end? I hardly thought Kyle was a better match than Calvin. The passion I felt with Kyle would surely turn to emotional turbulence and all kinds of other problems.

Lying in Kyle's bed while he sleeps I grip the covers in frustration. His chest rises and falls evenly, and I want to shake him for appearing so untroubled. He opens one eye and groans. 'What time is it?'

'It's late. Almost midnight.'

'Do you need to get going?'

'Do you *want* me to go?' I hate myself for sounding so insecure.

'C'mon Zoe, let's not do this.' He opens both eyes. 'What do you want? Life's short.'

I sigh. 'It'd all be easier if I knew where this was going.'

He places his hand on my leg. 'Are you asking if we'll get married? Live here together with the new baby?'

'Of course not.' I feel foolish.

'Let me ask you this—if anything were possible, what would you do?'

'It isn't that simple.'

'Isn't it? You'd rather do the right thing than be happy?'

'Yes. No. I don't know. I'm not sure that my life's so unfulfilling. Maybe I wouldn't be happy with anyone.'

He sulks and takes his hand away. 'So this isn't what you're looking for either.' His tone changes to become cold and sullen, like it used to whenever I displeased him.

My stomach turns. 'You're misunderstanding things.'

'Listen, stay if you want. I won't beg you.'

'You're hurt.'

'I guess so. I'm not sure what you expect from me.' He reaches for his jeans. 'I need to pee.'

My head drops onto the pillow. What had been affectionate between us now feels unfriendly. I'd forgotten this side of him—his tendency to go from hot to cold in an instant.

Last night I'd had a dream my teeth were falling out in bloody clumps. I woke up with an uneasy feeling that took most of the day to shake off. It didn't take a book on dream analysis to figure out I was panicked about losing something I couldn't get back.

He comes back and leans against the bureau. 'You need to figure things out. That's the thing about being a parent. It's not just about you anymore.'

'No kidding.' His hypocrisy annoys me. Ever since I'd seen the first ultrasound images of the baby I'd known there was someone else depending on me—even if I'd been scared to admit it.

The day Calvin and I visited the ultrasound clinic, a warm chinook blew into the city. From my west bedroom window I'd seen the chinook arch of blue sky topped by a vault of white clouds. But mostly I knew the winds were changing because I'd been more anxious than usual, and could sense a migraine coming on that had nothing to do with my visit to the clinic that afternoon.

The receptionist had commented: 'How's the weather?' As the temperature rose by several degrees in just a few hours, and the snow quickly melted, the chinook would be the main topic of conversation all day.

'The weather's fine,' I replied, rubbing my temple. Couldn't the receptionist see I didn't want to talk?

'They're ready for you.' She motioned for me to follow. 'Slip this on.' She handed me a robe. 'Everything off from the waist up.'

'My husband's meeting me—'

'I'll bring him back, don't worry. I imagine he'll want to see what's going on.'

'Yes.' He would be racing downtown in his Pathfinder, eager to get here.

Calvin arrived in time to watch the sonographer push the ultrasound wand across the cool gel that coated my bare belly. He stood at the head of the examination table, his arms folded across his chest while he rocked back and forth on his heels. So far I'd felt nothing. No quickening, no nausea. If I could ignore what was going on in my body I wouldn't have to deal with the apprehension of childbirth that bobbed to the surface every time I passed a pregnant woman. There were expectant women everywhere, it seemed. Calgary was in the middle of a maternity boom. Women were being sent to hospitals in High River and Okotoks to deliver. The health care system was bulging under the weight of so many babies.

The ultrasound wand slid to rest as if it were a canoe gliding noiselessly into shore. 'Look.' The sonographer pointed at the screen, pleased to have found what she was looking for so quickly. Without warning, the fetus came into view, its crater-like eyes glaring at us as if it were an alien from a low-budget movie. 'It's too early to tell the gender,' she told us. 'But there's your baby.'

'Hey,' said Calvin. He punched excitedly at my shoulder. 'Would you look at that?'

The alien moved its thumb to its mouth, its fingers fanning out in a wave.

'How does it breathe?' I asked dumbly.

She smiled as though she'd heard the question a hundred times: 'The baby's breathing amniotic fluid to develop its lungs. But the oxygen comes from the umbilical cord. It's quite amazing, when you think about it.'

Until then I hadn't fully comprehended that I was *with child*. The act of Calvin throwing his leg over mine and casually kneading my breast—which qualified as foreplay on days when we were both tired and had to get up early—couldn't possibly have led to something so life altering, could it? I had to admit, it did seem like a miracle. But my momentary feeling of wonder was overshadowed by anxiety.

I recoiled as the sonographer touched my hand. 'Everything looks just fine,' she said reassuringly, moving the wand around and pushing a button on her machine to record images for the radiologist to analyze later. 'Nothing to worry about, I'd guess.'

'It'll be okay, babe,' said Calvin. 'You'll see.' His tone was similar to the one he used with his patients before he injected their gums with a syringe.

'It's okay to be nervous.' The sonographer smiled.

'I guess there's no way to back out of this now.' I could tell by the way she and Calvin glanced at each other that my joke had fallen flat. I'd only meant to make light of my fear.

On the screen the alien rolled onto its back and away so we could no longer see its face. The sonographer removed the wand and turned the overhead light on. She mopped up the gel from my skin with a paper towel. 'I imagine you'll want prints.' She addressed Calvin instead of me. 'Most people do.'

Calvin cleared his throat and nodded. He waited until the woman left the room before speaking. 'Aren't you a little bit excited?'

I tugged at the zipper of my jeans. 'I think I'm just too tense to be excited. It's all so foreign.'

We stopped to pay for the prints, standing beside a pregnant woman with a stomach that hung over her stretchy waistband as if it were a balloon filled to bursting with water. The walls were plastered with posters of pregnant women beaming happy smiles, holding their bellies in a way that appeared to come naturally. You could be sure these women weren't smoking, forgetting to take their iron supplements, jogging up hills.

'Look.' He squeezed my shoulder. 'I know it'll be a transition. For both of us.'

'Thank you for realizing it.'

After the ultrasound I'd gone home and stretched out like a corpse in my bed. Calvin came in after a while to lie beside me. We were two cadavers lying side by side staring out the window at the brilliant blue of the chinook. I reached for Calvin's hand, letting him know I was sorry for not being more enthusiastic.

He turned toward me. 'I wish I could make you see that everything's going to be okay.'

'Aren't you worried about how things will change? We're used to going out for dinner whenever we want. Travelling. I don't want our lives to stop once the baby's here.'

'It won't be tough forever.'

I leaned my head on his shoulder. 'How do you know I won't be the world's worst mother to this baby?'

'Don't be silly.' He kissed the top of my head. 'You'll be great once the baby's here, I'm sure of it.'

Who is Kyle, who sits indifferently on the edge of his bed, to talk to me about sacrifice? Or to think his lifestyle is a model of good parenting? Suddenly I miss Calvin's calm steadfastness, the safety of being with him.

Kyle gets up and cracks his bedroom window open. 'You must feel something for the baby.'

'I don't know what I feel.'

I'd come back to Kyle sloppy with nostalgia and distressed about my future.

Then, suddenly, I feel something that troubles me more—a warm, wet sensation between my legs that signals something is very wrong.

Twenty-Two

'You're the father?' the admitting nurse at Concord General Hospital asks Kyle.

'No,' I reply for him. 'He's just a friend.' I see what the nurse must see—that it's one o'clock in the morning, and Kyle and I have been up to no good. My hair is messy, my lips swollen with recent intimacy. I resist placing my hands on my hair to smooth it down. Kyle's shirt is unevenly buttoned; he wears a cowboy hat to hide his own unruly hair. His feet are clad in runners without socks.

'We'll fill out your forms in a minute. First things first—are you bleeding right now?'

Kyle steps back, embarrassed.

'I think so, yes.' The maxi pad I'd found in my purse lies soaked with blood between my legs.

'Let's take your vitals.' The nurse wraps a blood pressure cuff expertly around my biceps. She is roughly my mother's age, but dressed in modern scrubs. Everything about her spells efficiency, from the immaculate white shoes to the cropped bob of silver hair. 'Have you been engaged in any activity that might bring on bleeding?'

'I'm not sure what you mean—'

She cuts me off sternly. 'Any physical activity that may have caused contractions.'

Kyle plays with loose change in his pockets.

My throat croaks out, 'You mean sex?'

'You've had sexual relations recently?' She glances up from the cuff.

'Yes,' I answer, full of shame. The pregnancy books had talked about bleeding but I'd paid little attention, concerned more with frivolous topics such as hair dye and over-hot bathwater. 'Could that have brought on the bleeding?'

'It's unlikely.' The nurse unwraps the cuff swiftly. 'Have you been lifting heavy objects.'

I think about all the boxes I've been carrying. Why had I been so confident nothing bad would happen? Or, more disturbingly, had a part of me been reckless on purpose?

The nurse continues. 'You'll have to wait for the doctor to examine you. He's dealing with a motorcycle accident right now. You're stable, but you still need to be seen as soon as possible.' She hands me a clipboard thick with forms.

'What do you think is wrong?'

'It's hard to say yet. You'll need a proper examination.' She looks down at my form. 'Zoe Lemonopolous. You must be Costa and Sophie's girl. The eldest?'

I nod, now recognizing the nurse as a friend of my parents from Rotary Club.

She narrows her eyes. 'You want me to call them?'

I shake my head, mortified. My parents will be humiliated to be told I'm pregnant over the telephone—and devastated to find me here with a man who isn't my husband. They'll guess everything. 'I don't want to worry them.'

She takes back the clipboard and clicks her pen shut sharply. She replies, doubtful, 'If that's what you want.

I nod.

'Visiting from Calgary, right? I don't imagine you expected this.'

'No.' I look at Kyle who stands off to the side. 'No, I didn't expect this.'

She takes the arms of my wheelchair and begins pushing. 'Many pregnancies terminate in the first trimester. Or even the second. I'll be honest. You're not far enough along for the baby to survive if there's a problem.' She wheels me into a room and helps me into bed. She hands me a box of maxi pads and draws a curtain around the bed. 'Don't get up unless you need to. I have to get back to my station. Press the button if anything changes. You'll likely want your mother soon.'

I shake my head. My insides contract in cramps that are far worse than any menstrual pain.

The nurse turns on her heel and leaves.

'Should I go?' asks Kyle, standing inside the bed curtain. It's obvious, by the way he stands as far away from me as he can in this small space, that he wants to get out before he's forced to get involved, just as he got out that awful night twenty years ago—

That night I'd finally coaxed my sister into a soapy bath. She'd been too distraught to be embarrassed as I helped her take off her nightgown. I found a washcloth in a drawer and dipped it in the bathwater, sponging her shoulders and arms. When I dunked the cloth between her legs she pushed my hand away.

I washed her back, making useless circles with the washcloth and listening for the sound of the front door. If my parents found us like this they would demand an explanation. If they'd been displeased with me in the past, it would be nothing compared to their fury over what had happened. I couldn't even guess what they would do and say.

Dorothea curled her knees into her chest, shaking.

I turned the hot water tap all the way to the right. 'Don't worry, it'll be okay,' I said, even though I myself could barely move, so paralyzing were my feelings of guilt and fear and confusion. I sat on the edge of the tub, dazed. The image of Cam lying on my sister crowded my thoughts, as I imagined his breath hot against her neck while his greedy hands pushed up her nightgown. Had it happened on the rumpus room sofa against my mother's throw cushions? Or had he followed her to the bedroom, ignoring her pleas while he crawled into her bed, kicking away the pink-striped pillows to make room? Had she tried to push him away only to be overtaken by the straitjacket of his arms? And afterwards—had he tried to kiss her, telling himself she'd enjoyed it?

I wrapped a towel around Dorothea and helped her out of the bath. She lifted her arms in the air so I could pull fresh pyjamas over her head as though she were a child. Even as I dressed her, she still refused to talk to me. I rinsed the Snow White nightgown in the bathroom sink and wrung it out.

My thoughts came joltingly—what would happen to us all, after this? When Dorothea finally talked, what would she say? If I'd been disconnected from my sister before, now any last threads holding us together would be broken.

My mother noticed the untidy state of the bathroom as soon as she got home. 'What have you girls been up to?' she asked, coming down to the rumpus room with the wet nightgown in her hand as evidence. We sat huddled together on the sofa under the afghan watching a *Laverne & Shirley* rerun. She narrowed her eyes at Dorothea. 'Are you all right?' She touched Dorothea's pale forehead. 'You look like a disaster.'

Dorothea stared mutely at the television while I held my breath waiting for her response. The laugh track from the television boomed, out of place.

'Well, I'm not sure what happened here, exactly.' My mother turned and went back upstairs, calling behind to us, 'Next time don't leave things in such a mess. And get yourselves to bed.'

That night I fell into a fretful sleep, waking often to thoughts of what might have happened. My mind came at the incident sideways, touching on it briefly like a bird trying to land on a crumbling ledge. I told myself it was a bad dream, it hadn't really happened. Then I was overtaken by the horror and pulled the covers up to my ears.

The next morning I'd woken early to the sound of a neighbour's dog barking, and had gone into my sister's bedroom.

She opened her eyes, startled.

'It's okay.' I touched her arm. 'Go back to sleep.'

'Does Mom know?' she whispered.

I shook my head. 'Do you want me to tell her?'

'I don't want to talk about it ever again,' she said, rolling away from me into her pillow.

I was ashamed to feel such relief.

On Saturday I found Kyle at the trailer court. When I told him what had happened, he'd been disbelieving, and tried to turn the conversation around. 'Are you sure your sister told you the whole story? You never got Cam's side.'

'Are you *kidding* me?' I was angrier than I'd ever been at him. '*You're taking his side?*'

He sat down on the trailer's rickety stairs and yanked a limp dandelion from between the steps. 'You're sure about this?'

I pulled the weed away from his hands and threw it on the ground, hissing, 'Yes, I'm sure.'

My rage, white-hot and seething, flustered him. He slumped back on his hands and sighed. 'That bastard.'

'You left me,' I reminded him, accusingly. 'You just left me there like you didn't care what had happened!'

'What was I supposed to do? Your parents were going to be home any minute.'

I nodded, but I was still bothered. I also knew by the way Kyle held himself apart from me that things were over with us. It wasn't that I blamed him—it was my responsibility to look after Dorothea, after all—but I could sense that this was too big for us to overcome, our guilt and shame opening up a vast distance between us.

After that horrible night, Cam disappeared. Someone heard he'd moved to Edmonton to live with his father, and someone else said he'd gone farther north to take a job planting trees. For a while there was talk about where he might be or why he might have left, but soon the chatter stopped. It was as though he'd never mattered that much to any of us. Besides, it was nearly the end of summer, and we were all moving toward different futures. Only Kyle and I knew why he'd gone, and we never said another word about him—not to each other, and not to anyone else.

I left for university a couple of weeks later, telling myself Dorothea's trauma would dull and that there was little I could do to fix things. I was ashamed to admit to myself that I still thought about Kyle. I promised myself I would come back home every weekend to check on my sister, but weekends turned into monthly visits, and those turned into holiday visits only, until I hardly ever came back. I'd thought being apart from my family would make things easier. But my absence meant Dorothea and I had never had the opportunity to move beyond that night.

Now Kyle stands holding the hospital-bed curtain, reluctant to be found out. In his dimly lit bedroom we'd been unconcerned about being caught. Here, in the bright lights of the hospital, we're exposed. The nurse will stick to the official code of confidentiality, of course. But in a small town like Concord, hospital corridors are hotbeds of gossip. Anyone could see us and guess the situation. News will travel.

'You should go,' I say. 'I'll call Dorothea.'

'You're sure?'

'It's better that way.' My eyes grow wet at his naked relief. What made me think he would act differently in this crisis?

He lingers as if to satisfy his conscience. 'You'll be okay?'

Bitterly I say, 'Just go.'

His eyes harden in an instant. I watch him disappear through the flimsy curtain, a swish of fabric, then stillness.

My stomach lurches. What had I expected from him? His paintings speak to his fickle nature. Canvas after canvas filled with images of abandonment that betray his troubled past: the farmwife running away from her home; the crows looking down hungrily on the busy world that ignores them; the madwoman leaning over her sleeping children with the threat of a knife in her hand.

We'd grown up together. We'd held each other when no one else was there, clinging to each other like life rafts, and we'd survived our adolescence because of it. We'd shared the thrill of our young bodies, and then we'd shared a terrible secret. These last few days I'd returned to him as though he could save me the way he'd saved me while we were young; I'd shoved aside thoughts of how he'd also deserted me back then, too.

The nurse pokes her head through the curtain after Kyle is gone. 'Oh,' she says, her manner softening when she sees me crying. 'You're upset about the baby, that's very normal.' She pulls the curtain aside to take my temperature in an efficient manner that says she's seen it all.

'Yes.' I nod pitifully, sorely disillusioned by Kyle's lack of courage. But I'm disappointed most of all in myself, and shocked at the problems I've created. Now that I'm faced with the loss of the baby, I'm not sure losing it is at all what I'd wanted. I'd only wanted to be free of my misgivings.

Twenty-Three

Dorothea comes right away, and stands tensely beside my hospital bed holding a bottle of purified water.

'You came,' I say.

'Of course I came. Are you having any pain?'

I reach for the water. 'Some cramping still. What do Mom and Dad know?' Since Kyle left I've been alone with my thoughts: What in the world will I tell Calvin if there's anything wrong with the baby? He's so excited he's already begun collecting miniature hockey jerseys, convinced it's a boy.

The cramps have eased since I got into bed, giving way to spasms of self-hatred. I don't dare ask God for understanding—why would He bother with me?

'I didn't wake Mom. She'll hear Ryan if he gets up. I left a note.'

'Good.'

'They'll know about the baby soon enough.'

'I was planning to tell them,' I reply, defensive.

'Marnie called when you were out.' Her raised eyebrow is cocked sanctimoniously.

'I wasn't out with Marnie.'

'I figured that much. You were out with *him* again?'

'I didn't ask you here to make me feel worse.'

She narrows her eyes. 'I'm not trying to make you feel worse. But Jesus, Zoe. You're married. You're having a *baby*. What were you thinking?'

She moves to the window, as far away from me as the room allows, even though there's a chair beside my bed. I shift miserably in bed and observe my sister's tired face which shows all of its thirty-five years. Her mouth has settled into permanent frown lines.

She plays with the zipper of her jacket and gazes out the window. Outside, snow is falling in wet spring flakes that will melt with the morning sun. Inside the hospital it's quiet—then a microwave dings and the smell of someone's late-night dinner reaches the room. Affliction is illuminated in this brightly lit hospital late at night while most people—Calvin, my parents—are sleeping, unaware, in their beds. An ambulance passes the window suddenly with sirens blaring, on its way to transport more of the unlucky ones.

Dorothea opens her mouth and closes it, as though reconsidering what she's about to say.

'What is it?' I ask.

'Forget it.' She presses her lips together.

'If you've got something to say, then just say it.'

She hesitates for a moment, then zips her jacket to her chin purposefully before her words strike: 'It's like you want to lose the baby.'

My fingers twist the tie of my hospital gown. My sister—how dare she?—has touched on my unspoken fear. 'Go to hell,' I strike back.

She scowls and stands facing me, unrepentantly. 'Don't act wounded because you don't like what I have to say. You're acting like a teenager for Christ's sake. How selfish can you be?'

To my horror, tears fill my eyes. 'I called you only because there was no one else.'

She looks down at her feet, as she used to when we were young and I'd hurt her feelings. 'Let's just get through this.' She turns her head as though to say, *Enough*.

For a moment I hate my sister, as she stands at the window, unmovable. I lie back on my pillow and look up at the ceiling tiles, which are stained with water damage. Someone has taped a rainbow poster on the ceiling for patients who are confined to lying on their backs. The kindness of that stranger only makes me feel worse.

Dorothea takes off her jacket and turns to look out the window, her thin back hunched in rejection.

The sight of her shoulder blades poking through her shirt like fragile wings causes me to break open with the sudden memory of that awful night, when she lay in her Snow White nightgown, facing the wall and refusing to let me see. Just as it had then, her turning away fills me with unimaginable dread. Even though I hadn't known all the circumstances, I'd known nothing would be the same again.

I start crying.

Dorothea turns and stares at me with surprise.

Quickly the tears turn to sobs. Tears, hot and unwanted, spill from my eyes onto my cheeks. There's no stopping the trembling of my arms and legs. Even my chin trembles pathetically.

A moan comes from somewhere deep inside, revealing a weakness that terrifies me. My body, coiled like a spring for so long, has finally let go. All my reserve dissolving into a mess of tears.

Now Dorothea looks frightened. 'Take a deep breath.'

My breath keeps coming in fast hiccups. I try to take a deep breath but can only wail, 'I can't. I can't.'

She pulls nervously at her hair. 'Can't what?'

'I can't fight with you anymore.' I blindly tear another tissue from the box beside the bed. I've always hated when others cried, embarrassed by their indignity, and not knowing what to say to comfort them.

'Fine. But you need to figure out what you're doing.'

'You think I don't know that?'

'I don't know what you think. You can't possibly think he loves you.'

For a second I'm confused—does she mean Calvin, or Kyle? But of course she means Kyle. 'You don't really know him.' My words are feeble.

'For God's sake, Zoe. Him of all people? Even talking about him brings it all up again—' She stops speaking abruptly.

I stare at her, shocked by the turn of our conversation. For a long time I've avoided Dorothea, afraid of where our talking might take us. For years we've sidestepped that horrible night, filling in the gaps with dialogue that didn't touch on what was really being said. When Dorothea criticized me for not visiting home enough what she really meant was, *Yes, we've all disappointed each other, but family still shows up.*

When I made excuses on the phone, I didn't tell the truth either: *I don't know how to be in your presence without the veil of what happened dropping between us. When I don't look you directly in the eye, it's because I don't want to see the reminder of my horrible betrayal.*

I answer weakly, 'I know you've been hurt.'

Dorothea stands looking out the window again. She is a pale reflection against the glass. She hugs herself tightly and stares at the snow. She doesn't turn toward me but I can see her expression is clouded. She plays with the unravelling hem of her sleeve.

I blubber, 'I know it was my fault, what happened with Cam.'

She places her hands upon the windowsill as though she needs to support herself. 'Say something,' I plead.

She keeps looking out the window at the parking lot. A truck passes our window. She turns to look at me finally, her eyes smudged with shadow. Her face, normally guarded, is bare, agonized: 'I *let* Cam kiss me.

And then it just ... went too far. I couldn't stop him.'

The words fall like stones, each one a heavy weight. The room fills with white noise at first. Then with the buzz of my anger at having been denied the full story for so long. I stare at my sister. She is gauging my reaction anxiously. She coils a strand of hair around her finger tightly, then notices that she's fidgeting and brings her hands together in a tight ball. Her frame is small and brittle against the window, as though the slightest tap would break her into pieces.

'It wasn't your fault,' I say wearily.

She looks down at her clenched hands. 'We've all messed up.' She frowns before continuing. 'But how can you be with Kyle Lipinski, and ignore the rest of us?'

I open my mouth to speak, then close it.

She shrugs. 'Maybe it's easier for you to pretend I don't exist.'

She wipes her eyes with her sleeve and stares dismally at the falling snow.

I look down at my lap, ashamed.

In her corner of the room she seems so alone. How could I not have seen what she really wanted? Then, as though to mirror my distress, the hospital intercom bleats out a code red. There is a flurry of carts and nurses in blue uniforms in the corridor, then all is calm again.

Silence takes up the space of the room, seeping into corners and under chairs like a lulling gas. The only sound is my pitiful sniffling. Finally Dorothea looks toward the door. 'That doctor is taking his sweet time.' It's the sort of comment meant to temper insults and hurts. A remark intended to say, *Let's pretend everything's fine.*

'Yes,' I croak gratefully. I look at the clock on the wall. The baby's fate, my fate, Calvin's fate—*our* fate—lies in this anonymous room.

Twenty-Four

In the end, the baby is fine. This shocks us all, including the doctor. What surprises me even more is my relief.

'You're lucky. The baby's heartbeat is still strong,' the doctor says, placing his cold Doppler wand on my belly one last time. 'This baby must be a survivor.' He looks at me, his eyes sharp with experience. 'You got lucky this time. You've probably been running around, making extra stress for yourself.'

Yes, I nod, disgraced. The rushing gallop of the baby's heart through the Doppler fills my eardrums. 'Does the heartbeat sound fast to you?' I ask the doctor. Dorothea stands by the bed watching.

'The heartbeat is fine. I'll let you go in the morning since the bleeding's stopped. But don't take any chances. You're at four months now, moving closer toward viability.'

I'd seen the mouselike babies in the neonatal ward in Calgary's Foothills hospital when I visited a friend of Frances's who'd delivered prematurely. Yes, I'd agreed too strenuously with the friend as we viewed the new baby through the glass window, the baby did look stronger than the rest.

I imagine my own baby now as a newborn mouse, its eyes bulging beneath skin as translucent as vellum, screwed closed against the intrusion of our worried voices. Distraught by its current circumstance, does it suck anxiously on its skinny thumb? A tug of concern, even a feeling of warm tenderness for the baby catches me by surprise.

I look down at my belly, acknowledging this sudden new emotion. I have a sense that it's less a change of heart than a moment of clarity, allowing me to recognize an impulse that already existed—I just didn't know it was there.

The doctor pulls my gown over my abdomen and steps back. 'Take care of yourself now.'

I nod my thanks.

Dorothea steps back, too. 'You got lucky,' she tells me.

'I did,' I reply, startled to find myself in this position, and also dazed with new thoughts—

It's as though I've stepped over a line, where the decision to feel—or not to feel—has been taken out of my hands. Emotions barely acknowledged are taking shape.

And there's something else pushing at me despite my weariness. A glimpse of an answer to what's been evading me: perhaps what I'd been interpreting all this time as despair about the baby has simply been fear—not fear that I wouldn't love the baby, but, rather, that I *would*.

In the past, I've denied connection, seeing love and rejection as two edges of the same blade. For the first time it seems possible that I might allow myself to trust that relationships can persist in spite of disagreement or hurt. I only have to think about Calvin, who in spite of his anger, our sharp words, and my petulance, has never walked away.

Even Dorothea seems more relaxed. 'I have to get back home.' Her voice has lost its edge. 'But I'll bring Mom and Dad in a few hours. Try to get some sleep.'

The rest of the night in the hospital passes in restless fits of dreams. When I wake up my sheets are clammy. The dawn sun filters weakly through the cracks in the window blinds, a pale amber haze that gradually fills the room like smoke, warning me that the trials of the day are about to begin. My pillow is flat and hard beneath my head. The string of my hospital gown pulls at my neck. I drift in and out of sleep, waking to the occasional ring of the nurse's station telephone.

Beneath the surface a memory—

I'm fifteen years old and swimming in Bitter Lake. My sister floats nearby while my mother lies on a towel in her red bikini reading *Chatelaine* magazine. I drift on my back, gliding beneath clouds as puffy as whipped cream. Gulls squawk as they dive down to gather silver minnows in their beaks. The tall trees of the shoreline glimmer in the lake's reflection. My father paddles over and grabs our toes, pulling us down into the water. My sister coughs, sucking in water and flailing out for my help, taken by surprise. 'It's all right.' Dad laughs, gathering us into the circle of his tanned powerful arms.

When did I lose my faith in others?

Had there been a moment of decision or had it happened slowly, disappointment and guilt pulling me away from those who loved me most?

I wake fully, disoriented for a moment. Such moments always bring me back to the past, when I would wake up as a child, confused, only to remember my parents were nearby. The morning light reaches my clothes hanging off the edge of the hospital chair like a traveller's. The messiness of my current life comes back to me.

By now my parents will be awake, listening with confusion and dismay as Dorothea tells them the events of the past night. They will come at once, hurt and wanting to understand why I've kept the pregnancy a secret. Calvin will need to be phoned; he'll answer in a groggy Sunday-morning voice that quickly grows alarmed. There will be questions to be answered, lies to be told.

I push myself out of bed, to the bathroom, and catch a look at myself in the mirror. What a wreck.

I pull my hair back with my hands and attempt a half-hearted smile. I read somewhere that the act of smiling creates a feedback loop whereby you actually feel happier as a result. Perhaps it's always been that simple but I didn't know it—just act the way you'd like to feel, until it becomes reality.

I wash my face in the sink, drying it with a rough paper towel from the dispenser. My skin is red and blotchy from crying. Whenever I cried as a child, my mother would produce a warm soapy facecloth to wash away the tears. She had a solution for everything: 'When you don't like what life hands you, you've always got another choice to make.'

'But how do I know what my choices are?'

'It's simple. You look at what's bothering you, and go in the other direction.'

Have I really believed my problems could be solved simply by turning away?

It makes sense that I've made a career of purging. It's what I know best—worries stowed under the bed so as not to be stumbled over. People set aside as easily as empty plastic containers. Memories stored away like faded photographs neatly boxed up in an attic. All reminders of my failings and regrets batched in tight, out-of-the-way bundles for fear they would trip me up for good.

My belly contracts, then releases. A reminder that some things can't be tossed aside.

I look closer in the mirror as though my reflection will magically utter the solution to my vexing nature. All I see are the same two hazel eyes, the slightly upturned nose, the mouth set in a silent pink line. The difference, I suppose, is that I'm finally taking stock. In the past few days I've reached rock bottom, that impossibly hard ground where there are only two choices—stay at the bottom, letting life pass me by—or push up and away, toward the surface.

I shake my hair free of its stringiness, pinch my cheeks to bring colour to my face. In the small bathroom vanity is a miniature tube of toothpaste and a toothbrush wrapped in clear plastic. I squeeze a small blue bead of paste onto the brush and scape away the film that coats my teeth and tongue with a fierceness that surprises me, as though I'm eradicating the most harmful elements of my personality—apathy, neglect, isolation, ingratitude.

Twenty-Five

I've been home from the hospital only a few hours when I find the Hush Puppies box in the closet while looking for my old velour bathrobe. I pull it down, puzzled by the duct tape that holds it shut, until I realize it's the time capsule Dorothea and I made when we first moved to Concord, ripe with cabin fever one rainy weekend afternoon.

I smile in spite of my fatigue. I sit on the bed, remembering Calvin's worried voice over the telephone earlier this morning: 'Promise me you'll rest until I get there?' His tone reminded me that I was not alone.

My mother has been hovering near my bedroom door ever since bringing me home from the hospital.

It moves me, her concern. In youth I'd never known what to expect from my mother. Once, I'd come across her in the garden beating the living room rug with a wooden paddle, a chore she hated more than any other. I must have been distressed with my friends because I was feeling anxious in the way I did whenever I felt they were growing tired of me.

'Do you love me?' I'd asked.

She'd stopped beating and turned around, her face red from the exertion. She plucked a sweaty hair from her cheek and frowned. 'What's the matter with you?'

'Nothing. Forget it.' I'd backed away, crushed. It wasn't that I hadn't known she loved me, only that I needed at that moment to hear it said.

If Dorothea hadn't gone out with Ryan to take their last few boxes to their new apartment, I would've called her to come open the time capsule with me. My curiosity gets the better of me. I peel the tape off to find a tube of cherry Bonne Belle Lip Smacker, a folded *Raiders of the Lost Ark* movie poster, postage stamps of Lady Diana's wedding portrait, an Olivia Newton-John cassette tape and, unexpectedly, a Greek blue evil eye *mati*.

I recall we'd holed up in the rumpus room with a collection of our favourite possessions spread across the shag carpet—torn between keeping them for ourselves and putting them away in the box for some vaguely formed notion of the future. I put my nose to the shoebox to find there is no longer any scent from those days. Even the Lip Smacker has lost its essence. A single sob escapes from my throat.

My mother knocks. 'Are you all right?' she asks through the closed door.

When I don't answer, she comes in and sits on the edge of the bed. 'We're concerned about you.'

I place the Hush Puppies box beside me. 'I don't mean to worry you.'

'You're always so hard on yourself.' She runs a wrinkled hand over the bedspread, thinking for a moment before continuing. 'I always thought it was my fault, if you want to know the truth. I know I was hard on you when you were growing up. I guess I didn't realize how much until after you'd gone away, and then it was too late to do anything about it.' She gives me a slight smile as she twists her hands in her lap. 'Anyway, that's what mothers do. They blame themselves for their children's unhappiness. What's that saying? "A mother is only as happy as her unhappiest child."'

'I guess I've made you pretty miserable, then.'

'Only because I don't understand why you're so troubled. It seems to me there's plenty to be happy about. I know you're anxious about the baby, but that's normal. You may surprise yourself when the baby comes. You've always been very natural with Ryan. I know he's not your own, and I'm not saying it isn't frightening to think you'll be responsible for a tiny baby. They say it's the most natural thing, being a mother. But it doesn't come easily for every woman. God knows I struggled myself.'

I nod.

She says carefully, 'I've learned the hard way that if you don't appreciate what's right in front of you, right when it's happening, your whole life will pass you by with little reward.'

Her admission catches me by surprise. Is it possible that my mother, who's always seemed so dissatisfied, has finally figured it out? Had anyone asked me, I would have said she wasn't the sort to think about such things.

'Well'—she pats my leg and rises to leave—'there's nothing that time won't fix. Another thing I've learned.'

Time. So much time to find my way.

I take the blue glass *mati*, which is meant to deflect bad luck, from the Hush Puppies box and turn it in my hands. On one side the painted white eye, on the other a smooth blank surface. Nothing more than a cheap piece of stone. I know very well that, like all charms, its significance comes not from the object itself but from the faith you bring to it. I shake my head, thinking, *It's just a stone and some paint.* But I slip it into the pocket of my robe just the same.

Twenty-Six

Calvin finally arrives at my parents' house, having driven all morning to get here.

'You're all right?' He sits beside me anxiously on the bedspread.

'I'm all right,' I say. 'Just tired.'

'You had me frightened. The thought of anything happening to you—'

'It didn't,' I interrupt him.

'But if it did.' He frowns.

In the hallway my mother fusses about the boxes to be taken to the Goodwill. 'I didn't get a chance to go through these,' she complains to herself.

I call from my bed, 'For goodness' sake, Mom, that box is for charity. Everything worth taking has already gone with the movers.' I force myself to talk in a milder tone. 'There's nothing of value in there, I promise. If you need anything once you're in the seniors' home, we'll get it for you.'

'It's not a seniors' home, it's an adult villa.'

Calvin and I can't help but smile at each other.

An hour later the Goodwill truck comes for the unwanted furniture—the La-Z-Boy, the worn rumpus room sofa, my parents' bedroom suite, which won't fit in the villa. The two men from Goodwill pick up most of the pieces easily, grunting only with the heavy sofa. They even take my bed, leaving the sheets on the floor. I bend carefully to gather them up; Calvin will be cross with me if he thinks I'm pushing myself.

I wander into the living room. The floors have been vacuumed into neat vertical stripes, the drapes pulled shut until the new owners arrive. Now that the rooms are empty it seems we've never lived here. I lift a drape and peer outside the kitchen window where the Greek flag no longer hangs. I suppose my father will hang it stubbornly outside his new window, arguing with anyone who tells him it doesn't conform to villa bylaws. *Goddamn Canadians*, he will criticize—*always with their rules*.

My stomach rumbles, reminding me to feed the baby. I take the apple and leftover hospital sandwich I find in the fridge to the living room and sit on the floor. Looking around the room I notice the wallpaper is gaping open at a seam. I rise and walk to it, slipping a finger in the gap to touch the orange-sunburst-patterned wallpaper my mother papered over when we moved to Concord, as soon as she could afford to—

'Why are you doing that today?' my father had asked, exasperated by her working in such hot weather.

'I didn't know it was going to be so hot.' She wiped the sweat off her upper lip with the back of her pink rubber glove and held a strip of wallpaper high above her head. 'I need the stool.'

'Here.' My father dragged the stool over.

'Put it under my feet.'

He slid the stool closer to her and stepped back. 'You want a hand doing that?'

'You have to ask?' she replied, annoyed. 'Hurry, the paper's going to dry.'

I knew the situation would end with my mother barking orders and my father storming out of the room, muttering, *There was nothing wrong with the old wallpaper. You gotta change everything!*

'C'mon,' I'd said to Dorothea, who sat on the stairs watching. 'Let's get out of here.'

Working quickly together, my parents stuck the wet strip of paper to the wall. 'We got it!' my mother said triumphantly, patting it down with her hand. 'Wasn't that easy?'

My father nodded and stepped back to look at the finished pattern. But the strip of wallpaper tore away from the wall, bringing with it several strips of paper that shrouded my parents like ghosts.

I held my breath waiting for my father to blow up. Dorothea jumped up from the step. There was silence, then giggling from under the wallpaper, and finally howls of laughter as they freed themselves from the wet paper.

In the end my father finished the job. 'Not bad, eh?' He called us into the room to admire his handiwork.

'Not bad,' my mother agreed, putting her arms around our shoulders.

Later we replayed the event at the dinner table, cracking up all over again as happy families do.

Soon the curtains of the house will be drawn for the new owners, the front door locked and double-checked behind us. Calvin has to work tomorrow, so we'll be on our way home to Calgary this evening once we've seen that my parents are properly settled in at the Vista Grande.

The next time I come back to Concord it will be to Villa Grande, with light switches in unfamiliar places and floorboards that don't groan. How many times have I yanked on the sticky front door of my youth, so that every other door since then has been pulled with more force than necessary? Memory, like the stubborn door, makes us cling to futile habits.

My parents and Dorothea stand behind the screen door of their new apartment watching us get into Calvin's Pathfinder to make the drive home to Calgary. My mother's once-fashionable teal pants are obscured by the screen. When I was growing up, my mother took pride in being stylish in spite of having to wear a restaurant uniform most days. Nowadays her lipstick is too orange, and her eyebrows are pencilled on in an arch that causes her to appear startled. I think, *Good for her for still making an effort.*

I'd allowed myself to lean into her shoulder before leaving, long enough to smell the spice of her perfume. I'd raised my eyebrows at Calvin as though to say, *Can you believe what you're seeing?* My mother and I hadn't embraced since I was nine years old and tearful about heading to the summer camp where I would spend two miserable weeks drinking warm apple juice and gluing moss into shoeboxes to make nature dioramas.

'Are you sure you don't want to stay the night in the spare room?' asked my mother worriedly.

'No,' I said, 'we have to get home.' We'd be back soon to collect my car, I reminded her. And for once even Dorothea hadn't scoffed at the suggestion that I might return.

I'd taken the mounted trout, which pleased my father. 'Be careful with that,' he'd said as he helped me load the box into the space between the front seats. 'You remember how hard it was to catch that slippery devil.'

'Take it easy,' Calvin cautions as he helps me into the Pathfinder for the ride home. I take his arm, allowing myself to be hoisted into the warm cab of the truck. I pull my seat belt around my hips and secure its clasp, looking up to wave goodbye to my parents.

My father stands beside my mother like a tower. For years he's carried so many burdens in a stern manner that appeared uncaring—the difficult years with the restaurant, the brewing trouble of teenagers and now his health worries. He's never let us down, providing the means to a comfortable life without fail.

And my mother? She's put up with years of mockery at her efforts to better herself, without us noticing how well she'd also tended our home and our lives. My eyes tear up at the way we've all misunderstood, and mistreated, one another.

Now I'm on the road with Calvin and the baby—this family I've created in spite of my tendency for solitude.

I watch through the truck window, which steams up from my breath and wipe the glass with my sleeve like a child. A Handi-Van jerks its way down the road ahead of us—carrying a load of seniors to the bingo hall, or maybe to the Seniors' Friendship Centre.

I take in the local landmarks—the tidy row of evergreens planted for the province's centennial anniversary in 1967, the year I was born. The handmade signs and larger billboards advertising small-town businesses: THE WELL COME INN. STYLES N' SMILES HAIR SALON. NATIVE ARTIFACTS LOCATED BEHIND PIZZA HUT.

Calvin drives slowly. 'I can't believe you grew up here. Does everyone wear a baseball cap?'

'Don't be a snob.'

'All right. But Christ, it's so bleak.'

'It's the weather,' I say.

Calvin turns onto the Chinese pavement. 'I thought we'd take a short-cut.'

'Watch the loose gravel.'

'I'll drive slowly, it won't damage the truck.' Normally he'd be uptight about the gravel, and would be short with me as a result, but the trials of the last twenty-four hours have made us gentle with each other.

The Chinese pavement leads to farming acreages populated by bungalows with oversized garages and decorative wishing wells. In summertime the wells hold sturdy pink hydrangea, splinters of tiger grass, snapdragons that cling by their tentacles to chicken wire.

A farmer's truck slows as it approaches; the driver waves a greeting. A car filled with teenagers speeds past, causing me to grip the door handle.

Calvin glances over. 'You all right?'

I nod, afraid of the sound my voice will make if I speak. He's asking about the baby, of course. He doesn't have a clue about the secret of Kyle that tightens in my gut like a slip knot.

I look in the rear passenger mirror where Concord has disappeared. 'Could you pull over? I need a breath of air.'

'We just got started. You need to be home taking it easy.'

'It won't take long.'

'All right,' he says doubtfully. 'As long as you know what you're doing.'

I look out the window and listen to the even tone of Calvin's voice. It's what I love most about him. His personality is rarely hot or cold, but rather a warm steady flow of energy I take for granted. If he's been displeased with me lately, he's had good reason.

I wonder what Calvin will say when I tell him the reason for the tension between Dorothea and me. I suspect he'll treat it like he treats everything else—with compassion. *You had no way of knowing what Cam would do*, he'll say. *Teenagers live in the here and now.*

No matter what, Calvin will never know about Kyle.

And what *of* Kyle? Is he a gash that will fade with time, becoming so imperceptible I'll have to look closely to see where the injury occurred? My throat tightens with the ache that comes from losing something you'd only ever imagined existed.

'This is where you want to stop?' Calvin asks as I direct him to pull over to the side of the road. 'There's nothing here.'

I pull at the door handle and step onto the road, which is wet with frost.

'Don't slip,' he warns.

The road is slick beneath my feet.

Calvin gets out and stands beside me looking at the disappearing sun. 'You okay?'

'Oh, yes, fine.' My voice is thick with emotion. My near brush with calamity has rattled my defences.

'You sound different than you have lately.'

'I do?'

'Yes, a bit.'

I see that I am worrying Calvin by standing here in the middle of nowhere. I draw a line with my boot in the frost, then erase it. 'I guess I'm feeling ... more ... aware of things than I have been.'

He looks at me oddly.

I continue with a short laugh. 'Not that I'm completely enlightened. But I do have a sense that things can improve.'

'That's good. Isn't it?'

'Yes. I've been so worried that my lack of maternal instinct means I won't be a good, or happy, mother.' I think about my next words carefully. 'This baby makes me feel so out of control. Like I'll mess everything up.'

'You won't mess it up.'

'I'd like to think so. I wish I had the sort of faith in myself that you do.' I give him a wry smile. 'Maybe I'm feeling a bit braver, that's all.'

He takes me by the arm, pleased. 'I'd say that's very good news.' He guides me toward the truck. 'Come on then. We need to get you off your feet.'

I allow him to help me into the truck. A week ago I would have resented his attention.

The radio is playing 'You Can't Always Get What You Want' by the Rolling Stones.

Calvin notices me smiling. 'What's so funny?'

'Nothing.' I shake my head.

Always cautious, Calvin flicks on the signal light although no traffic is visible for miles, and pulls back onto the road. A pothole jostles us forward. To our left, a traffic sign cautions: WATCH FOR LOOSE ROCKS. He reaches for my hand as though to reassure me he'll look out for me, no matter what.

I close my eyes, lulled by the rocking of the truck into the sort of sleep where you're not sure if you're awake or dreaming. On that drive home with Kyle on this same rocky road years ago, unaware of what was waiting ahead, I'd felt the night rich with summer and hope.

I open my eyes to find Calvin beside me in the Pathfinder. It's been twenty years since that night, and I see now what a waste I've made of time. Lacking an adult's perspective, I've blamed everyone else for my loneliness.

'You cold?' Calvin turns up the heat. He glances over and smiles his easy grin, the grin that had captivated me from the start. Why am I only really seeing it now?

In the distance, the bright orbs of the main highway's streetlights come into view. The road is busy with weekend traffic heading south, so many people returning to their lives.

We pick up speed as we pull onto the smooth black road.

The trout gapes up at us in frozen awe, our companion on this unaccustomed journey.

Acknowledgements

With many thanks to the following for literary encouragement, friendship, and teaching over the years: Anar Ali, Krista Ellingson, Athene Evans, Karen Hebb, Adrian Kelly, Rosemary Nixon, Cathy Ostlere, Anne Sorbie, Aritha van Herk, Gisèle Villeneuve.

With thanks, also, to my circle of friends outside the writing community for their interest and support of my work.

With gratitude to the team at The Porcupine's Quill for their dedicated professionalism, most notably publisher Elke Inkster for her cheerful enthusiasm and faith in *Bitter Lake*. With much appreciation to publisher Tim Inkster for his passionate commitment to the world of books. And to my editor, Chandra Wohleber, for her astute and invaluable editing; her steady support; and her kind gestures of friendship. A thank-you as well to Stephanie Small for her keen marketing efforts.

With acknowledgement to The Canada Council for the Arts and The Alberta Foundation for the Arts for their generous patronage of this project. Also, to the family of Brenda Strathern for its much appreciated support and recognition of Alberta writers.

With love to my family, especially my mother, Pamela Deliyannides, for unflagging dedication in every way. For Jacqueline Honnet, fellow author and friend of a lifetime, for seeing my novel through every page. For my children, Harris and Théa, who already understand the importance of a good story.

And for my husband, Paul Sali, who never doubts.

About the Author

Born in Edmonton to immigrant parents, Marika Deliyannides lived in Greece for a short time before moving back to Alberta at the age of six. Her family lived in a rural town that shares many similarities with the fictional town of Concord—including the nearby lake where teenagers cruised on summer nights. *Bitter Lake* is her literary debut. An excerpt of the book was awarded the Brenda Strathern Prize for most promising first fiction and was also published in *Alberta Views Magazine* as winner of its annual fiction contest.

Deliyannides is a graduate of the University of Alberta's English program, has published several short stories in literary magazines, and has been a business writer in Edmonton and Calgary, producing magazine articles, business copy and speeches.

She lives with her husband and two children, working from her home office overlooking the oil and gas towers of downtown Calgary.